A KISS FOR MISS HAMILTON

Owen captured Pen in the darkened hallway, grabbing the candle from her with one hand and seizing her shoulder with the other.

"What are you doing?" he demanded. "What business have you in the east wing that I should continually find you here?"

Pen didn't think her heart would ever recover from the shock he had given her, but she was m___ ___cerned about the grip b___ ___der. "Owen, you are ___

"Not as much as y___ actually trusted you! T___

Anger and a deep se___ ___he him. There standing b___ ___him, already within his grasp, was the one person he held responsible for such emotions. Before he knew it, before he even realized his own intentions, he had caught her in a crushing embrace and was kissing her.

Pen couldn't get away and she couldn't make him stop. She could only hope that if she succumbed to his kisses, he might let her go.

No sooner did her struggles cease than the tenor of his kiss changed. Gone was the bruising pressure of his mouth against hers. Instead, his lips softened and seemed to coax from hers a response that was very near a piercing sweetness. His lips kissed and teased hers, leaving her feeling breathless and exhilarated and desperate to have him kiss her yet again . . . .

Books by Nancy Lawrence

DELIGHTFUL DECEPTION
A SCANDALOUS SEASON
ONCE UPON A CHRISTMAS
A NOBLE ROGUE
MISS HAMILTON'S HERO

Published by Zebra Books

MISS HAMILTON'S HERO

Nancy Lawrence

Zebra Books
Kensington Publishing Corp.

http://www.zebrabooks.com

ZEBRA BOOKS are published by

Kensington Publishing Corp.
850 Third Avenue
New York, NY 10022

First Printing: March, 1999
10 9 8 7 6 5 4 3 2 1

Printed in the United States of America

To Sherrie Starts,
a special sister

ACKNOWLEDGMENTS

I owe a special debt of gratitude to Romance Writers of America (RWA). The many writers and contributors who make up RWA's ranks are unfailingly generous in their support of writers of all levels of expertise. I am pleased and proud to be a member of this organization.

Special thanks must also be given to my ever-constant and always-loving support group: Melanie Brunson, Debbie Gunderson, and Wyona Starts.

Chapter One

The outmoded carriage bearing the Hamilton coat of arms bumped and jolted its way down the Brighton Road. In it, Miss Penelope Hamilton, having almost abandoned all her fantasies concerning the excitement of travel, stared listlessly out the window at the passing countryside still visible in the gathering dusk of the June day.

After a long while, in which the only sights that greeted her eyes were still more trees and bushes and cart tracks, Penelope said, rather to herself, "I wish we would be set upon by footpads."

Her maid, who had succumbed to the boredom of their journey and had just fallen to dozing gently on the seat opposite her mistress, jolted awake at this and said in some alarm, "Oh, no, miss! Lud! Why ever would a nice young lady like you wish for such a thing?"

"A footpad might at least provide us with some interest," said Pen, directing a look of wide, brown-eyed innocence her direction.

"Before or after he was to slit our throats, I should like to know?" retorted her maid severely. "Highwaymen and road agents represent the vilest form of humanity, Miss Pen, capable of the most odious behavior! Why, I have heard tales that would curl your ears!"

"But Betty, I shouldn't wish to be murdered. I should only wish to be robbed," said Pen reasonably. "Before I arrive at Grandmama's house, I should like *some*thing of interest to occur. I've lived all of my nineteen years in quiet, circumspect, and boring seclusion. Nothing exciting ever happens to me or to my neighbors, or, indeed, to anyone of my acquaintance."

"And that is as it should be," said Betty firmly. She gave an indignant sniff. "Your dear aunt has raised you to be a nice young lady of breeding and proper heritage, and I think she would faint dead away to hear you speaking such nonsense. Excitement, indeed! Talk like that, Miss Pen Hamilton, shall earn you a reputation as an adventuress!"

Pen was fairly well convinced that no such epithet would ever be attached to her name. Indeed, her entire journey to Brighton was proving to be one of decided boredom. That, thought Pen, was a good deal too bad. She had left her aunt's home with the highest hopes for adventure, and it was a matter of deep disappointment to her that she would most likely arrive at her grandmother's estate at Brighton without having experienced the smallest incident.

At the least, Pen had hoped to meet some person of interest along the way. She had not. At the most, she had thought her coach might have been set upon by footpads; it now appeared that she would not have the pleasure of experiencing that event, either.

To have been robbed at gunpoint on the Brighton Road was an event not uncommon. Certainly, Pen's aunt had considered just such a possibility, for no sooner had the dear woman favored Pen with a quick hug and tucked her securely within the confines of the ponderous old carriage than dear Aunt Jane had stepped away to speak in hushed tones to her aged coachman. Oh, her words had been low, and she had obviously not wished for Pen to overhear, but Pen *had*. She had listened to every word as dear Aunt Jane had regaled John Coachman with a severe lecture on his hallowed duty to protect her dear Pen from the horrid advances of any highway robber.

Pen quite heartily wished such a robber would present himself, if only to relieve the tedium of the jostling coach, if only to provide her with an experience of which she might proudly and importantly tell her grandmother upon her arrival in Brighton.

But her wish had not been granted. Already, Pen thought she could see the spires of The Marine Pavilion in Brighton, fast approaching through the carriage window. And so she guessed she was very near her destination and had accomplished her journey without mishap, without adventure, and without any marvels to tell of her trip.

An idle, rather dejected glance out of the window told Pen that they were traveling up a small rise lined on either side with a dense thicket of trees and bushes. The coach, of necessity, slowed its pace as it negotiated the incline in the road. As it did so, Pen caught the sound of horses galloping out of sync, horses other than those that were drawing the coach.

Everything happened very quickly after that. No sooner did Pen realize that there must be another rider on the road than her carriage lurched to a halt. A pistol sounded, Betty let loose a yelp of terror, and a chorus of shouting male voices pierced the twilight.

Pen's heart beat a little faster. Her wish had come true—they were being set upon by a highwayman! She sat up a bit straighter, looked avidly out the window, and blessed what little there was of the remaining daylight that she would be able to see with hazy but sufficient clarity the exciting drama about to unfold.

The carriage door flew open and a deep, masculine voice commanded, "Madam, you will be good enough to step down!"

Betty let loose another piercing scream and shrank back against the carriage, but Pen, made of much sterner stuff, leaned forward and paused just in the door frame of the carriage. Looking up, she stared straight into the eyes of a highwayman.

He was still astride his horse, a large, magnificent beast of no less than sixteen hands that stamped and fidgeted beneath him as if it were impatient to be off. The animal added to the overall effect of a man to be reckoned with: dark and powerful and a little bit dangerous.

A black mask covered most of the highwayman's face, but Pen could see the square, masculine line of his jaw and the hint of black curls peeking from beneath his hat. A greatcoat shrouded his shoulders and hung in folds past the trim, muscled length of his legs.

The highwayman held a pistol in one hand and a saber in the other, and when he rose up in his stirrups and waved his gun slightly in her direction, Pen felt her lips go suddenly dry.

"Madam," he said, in his deep voice, "be pleased to step down. It is not a good thing to make me await your presence. For you see, time is of the essence in my position."

He thrust his pistol into the waistband of his pants and leaned down to hold out his hand to her.

She hesitated only a moment. There was something about him, some quality she could not quite name, that told Pen she had nothing to fear from this masked stranger. Slowly at first, then more confidently, she reached out and placed her hand in his, then stepped lightly down from the carriage.

She withdrew her hand and looked up at him, an expression of shining wonder on her face. "Why . . . why, you're a gentleman! And you are very gallant, even if you do intend to rob me!"

His finely-chiseled lips parted into a wry little smile and he straightened in his saddle, the better to examine Pen's brown eyes and brown curls as they peeped from beneath the brim of her bonnet. He apparently liked what he saw of her, for his smile grew slightly and he sketched a short bow from his saddle.

"To a little brown wren my conduct shall be ever gallant, but my good manners must not prevent me taking what I want."

"You speak very oddly," she said, having noticed a certain cadence to his words. "I cannot detect an accent but there is something . . . please, won't you say something else to me? Won't you speak again?"

There was a decided glint in his eyes behind his mask. "Alas, when next I speak I must demand from you your treasure, although to do so can bring me no pleasure!"

"Why, you speak in rhyme!" she murmured, as intrigued by that sudden realization as she was by his enchanting smile. "Tell me why you do so!"

He laughed slightly. "Tell you why I speak in rhyme? Such tales must await another time. For now, little brown wren, your jewels I demand. Place them, I beg you, here in my hand."

"But you are so clever! I quite forgive you, and I shan't scold you for robbing me," said Pen generously. She stepped back up into the doorway of the carriage and reached across her cowering maid to fetch a small traveling case that was resting upon the cushioned seat. She turned back to him and opened the case, saying, "I haven't many jewels, just a few that I inherited from my mother. I . . . I hope you shall not think ill of me for it."

He shook his head slightly and moved his fretting horse forward, holding out his hand to her. Into it Pen placed a string of pearls that had once belonged to her mother and a pair of topaz earrings that her aunt Jane had proudly presented to her on the occasion of her eighteenth birthday. "I am afraid they are not very expensive jewels, but they have great value to me, in a sentimental way. You . . . you will take good care of them, won't you?"

"Their value is no less because I possess them now, but they will be put to better use, I vow." He tucked the jewels into a pocket in his greatcoat.

Pen looked up into his masked face and found herself wondering what features he hid behind that length of black silk. She had a notion that he was a very handsome man. He was certainly gallant, curiously gentle, and decidedly intriguing. And when he looked down at her—standing poised upon the top step of the coach—and smiled just slightly, she felt her heart swell with some curious, unnamed emotion.

"Please, won't you tell me what circumstances in your life brought you to such a pass? Tell me how a gentleman such as you was forced into such a vile occupation!"

His smile increased, as did the pull of attraction Pen felt for him. "Vile?" he repeated. "No, that cannot be true! No occupation may be vile if it brings me to you."

She blushed rosily in the gathering moonlight. "That . . . that is quite the nicest thing anyone has ever said to me!"

He laughed softly and watched her thoughtfully for a moment. Then he sidled his mincing horse closer to where she stood poised upon the step. His gloved hand reached out to her and gently captured her chin, forcing it up.

Pen felt the flush in her cheeks deepen as he took his time, examining every detail of her face. From above his mask his gaze was thoughtful, and there was again that hint of a smile that shaped his lips. He swept his hat from his head, and his black curls shone silver in the moonlight. Slowly, he leaned forward until his lips found hers.

It was, Pen thought, a moment of exquisite madness, and she knew herself to be completely and utterly under his spell. She stood frozen on the step of the coach, feeling the light brush of his lips upon hers, until at last he gently released her.

She looked up at him, her eyes like stars. "Shall . . . shall I ever see you again?" she asked in a breathless voice.

"I may make you no promise, as we part, except to say most truthfully, you have captured my heart."

"Have I?" she breathed, feeling herself go pink with pleasure.

He smiled at her again. Then he turned his horse about at the same time he withdrew the pistol from beneath the folds of his coat. His horse rose up and then caracoled dangerously as the highwayman wagged the pistol in the general direction of the coachman still cowering on the box.

"Driver, provide my little brown wren a gentle ride into Town!" he commanded of John Coachman. Then his horse sprang forward, and he disappeared into the trees on one side of the road.

Pen stood for some moments frozen upon the

coach step, wondering if he would return, wondering if it had all been a dream. When she heard a gasp and a moan emit from behind her, Pen knew she need doubt her senses no more.

She turned on the step and called up toward the box, "Drive on, John! Drive on!"

She didn't need to exhort her coachman a second time. Having recognized the peril of their situation the very same moment he had recognized that he was staring down the barrel of a highwayman's pistol, John Coachman hadn't so much as twitched a muscle during their entire encounter with the highwayman except to draw short, ragged breaths of air. He now desired to put as much distance as possible between himself and the highwayman who had threatened his life. He put the horses to with a lunge that threw Pen back against the cushioned seat of the old coach, and then set off down the road at an uncommonly furious pace, jostling his passengers most uncomfortably.

The jarring of the coach revived Betty a little. Pen claimed her limp and lifeless hand between her own and attempted to revive her still more. But for all her ministrations, Pen's thoughts remained on the daring, attractive highwayman. She patted Betty's fingers in a distracted, haphazard way, all the while recalling the feel of the highwayman's lips upon hers, the touch of his gloved fingers against her skin.

Pen had never been kissed before. Under the chaparonage of either her maid or her aunt Jane, she had never contrived to be alone with any of the young bucks who resided in her village. Now, however, she had a fairly good notion of what she had been missing.

Her senses were fluttering riotously, and she was feeling quite breathless yet inordinately strong—as if she were capable of stepping down from the coach and running on foot the remainder of the journey to Brighton. She was as unable to concentrate on the passing scenery, as she was virtually unaware of her maid's hand clasped in hers. Luckily, Betty's swoon was not of a deep variety. Pen did not have to employ her vial of smelling salts which, as her dear aunt Jane had often told her, no true lady of fashion was ever without.

John Coachman drove on in the gathering darkness at a fast and furious pace, and they arrived at their destination after dark. Rosemount, the home of Pen's grandmother, was situated some distance off the Brighton Road, less than two miles north of Town itself. John Coachman, still driving in something of a panic, took the turn off the Brighton Road at a speed so sharp that Pen was forced to clutch at the window frame to save herself from being thrown to the other side of the vehicle. The carriage swept up the long drive and came to a stop before a large, imposing country house.

At the top of a flight of wide steps the front door opened, and the light from the interior of the house spread toward the coach. Two footmen carrying lanterns and dressed in magnificent livery emerged from the house to throw open the carriage door and assist Pen down.

"Goodness! Is this Grandmama's house?" she asked, her brown eyes wide with wonder. She stepped down onto the neatly groomed drive and surveyed what she could of the impressive façade in the dim light of the lanterns. Betty, still feeling the effects of their journey but determined, nevertheless, to perform her duties, stepped down and weakly followed Pen up the steps into the majestic front hall.

A butler stepped forward to greet them, and two more liveried footmen accepted Pen's coat and muff. "Good evening, miss," said the butler. "Mrs. Kendrick is in the yellow salon."

To Pen, who had grown up under the care of an aunt who had employed only two maids and one manservant about the house, having so many attendants signified luxury, indeed. She followed the butler up the imposing flight of stairs to the first floor. Yet another footman threw open a door at their approach. Pen heard her name announced.

She stepped across the threshold, looked swiftly about, and formed the instant opinion that she had entered the most elegantly styled salon she had ever seen. Her first impression was of daffodils, for fragrant bouquets of that flower were arranged at various points about the room. The walls were covered in sunny yellow silk, and the windows were hung with a rich fabric of gold brocade. The mahogany furniture was delicately carved in the style of the day, and the chairs and settees, like the walls, were covered in rich silks.

At the far end of the room, seated in chairs drawn near to the fire, were a young woman of uncommon beauty and an older woman dressed quite stylishly in a gown of midnight blue. She was stroking a small, white dog as it lay in idle luxury upon her lap. At the sound of the door opening the woman's hand stayed, and she looked up to survey Pen for a moment in silence.

She stood, cradling the dog in the crook of one arm, and held out her hand to Pen. "How like your dear mother you look! She was quite lovely, too, you know. Now, come here my child, and let me kiss you!"

Pen felt her heart swell. In a rush, she went to her, her hands outstretched, exclaiming, "Oh, Grandmama! I have had *such* an adventure! You shall be astonished when I tell you!"

Chapter Two

Mrs. Kendrick was little prepared for the young woman who came rushing across the room toward her, her hands outstretched, and her expression aglow. For too many years had Mrs. Kendrick's imagination conjured up an image of a granddaughter raised in a country village by a spinster aunt who hailed from the more questionable side of the family. She had expected to greet a granddaughter of plain looks and demure manner; she had expected a granddaughter dressed in clothes that were outlandishly passé and unbearably dreary. Miss Penelope Hamilton, however, fit neither description.

Penelope's hair was a deep chestnut brown, arranged conservatively yet stylishly about her head. Her large, brown eyes, framed by long, dark lashes, were set above a straight nose and a small, pointed chin. Her manners were pleasing, her smile enchanting. All in all, the girl was much more than Mrs. Kendrick had ever dared hope.

She held Pen close for a moment and kissed her lightly upon the forehead. Then she laughed a light, quizzical laugh and said, "An adventure? Only a child who has lived her entire life in the country could think a carriage ride over bumpy roads an adventure!"

"Oh, but Grandmama! It was all most exciting! Only wait until I have told you!"

"All in good time, my dear, but first you must let me introduce you to another member of our little family. Augusta dear, come and greet your cousin Penelope."

Pen's attention swung from her grandmother to the other woman in the room, who rose to her feet and dipped a short curtsy.

Miss Augusta Berwick looked upon Pen with eyes the color of a cloudless spring sky. Her complexion was flawless, and she was generally accorded to be in possession of a stunning figure. Her gold-blonde hair was fashionably fringed about her face and brushed tenderly across her lightly flushing cheeks.

Pen shook her hand, all the while peering up into Augusta's lovely face. "Goodness! Are you my cousin Augusta? How beautiful you are!"

That unexpected compliment deepened the faint tinge of color in Miss Augusta Berwick's cheeks. Flustered but somehow laughing, she said, "Welcome to our home, Cousin Penelope. I hope you shall be very happy here."

As Augusta moved away to resume her seat, Pen

caught sight of a small, white dog nestled upon a collection of pillows on the settee.

"And who is this little one?" she asked, moving toward the dog. "Please, may I pick her up?"

Mrs. Kendrick scooped the little dog up and tenderly placed her in Pen's arms. "This is my Candace. She is never from my side . . . so devoted! She goes everywhere with me, simply everywhere!"

Pen sat down next to her grandmother, and her fingers found the spot behind Candace's ears that reduced the animal to a state of abject slavery. "What a magnificent place Rosemount is—much grander than I ever imagined. And you are all so handsome! How happy your lives must be!" She cast a sunny smile upon her cousin and grandmother, and they, in turn, smiled politely back.

"I'm sure we go on very comfortably," said Mrs. Kendrick. She patted her skirts invitingly, and Candace immediately moved back to her lap. "Of course, we don't entertain as often as we used to in the past, but I think we might be able to contrive one or two affairs that shall prove amusing for you."

"I should like that above all things, Grandmama. Before I left Aunt Jane she told me I must avail myself of any parties or gatherings I am able. If you will merely lend me your countenance, I promise I shall not be a burden to you in any way," said Pen earnestly.

"A burden?" repeated Mrs. Kendrick. "My dear, I am convinced you could never be any such thing."

"I hope you are right, but Aunt Jane told me I must be very careful in that regard, for orphans such as I have a tendency to be very trying. She said I must strive to be otherwise.''

For a moment Mrs. Kendrick said nothing, so touched was she by her granddaughter's words. It had never occurred to her that her poor, orphaned granddaughter might have been raised by a spinster aunt who was possessed of a less than kind disposition. Her heart swelled, and for a moment she didn't quite know which would bring her stronger satisfaction: to gather the poor girl into her arms and hold her close, or box Aunt Jane's ears. She resisted both notions with an effort, but still she was compelled to produce a delicate, lace kerchief and dab it at her misting eyes. "You poor orphaned child! How *can* you speak of being a burden when you must know you are no such thing! Why, it is my dearest wish to have you here with me and your cousins. No, you must never speak of being a burden! You must concentrate instead only on enjoying all the entertainments put before you. I hope you shall be very happy here, my dear.''

"I'm sure I shall be," Pen said confidently. "Tell me, Grandmama—these entertainments you are planning . . . shall they be small affairs, such as card parties? Or very large entertainments, such as . . . say, a ball, perhaps?''

Mrs. Kendrick ceased plying her lace kerchief to her eyes and cast Pen a blank look. "A . . . a ball?''

"Yes, ma'am. You see, I should much prefer to attend a ball. And please, may it be a ball with a supper?''

Mrs. Kendrick looked from Pen to Augusta, then

back to Pen. "A . . . a supper?" she echoed, not at all certain she had heard correctly.

"Yes, ma'am. A ball with a supper and a good number of nobility, too, if you please. I should very much like to meet an earl, or at the very least a viscount."

This pronouncement was followed by a moment of quiet as Mrs. Kendrick and Augusta each looked upon Pen with increasing confusion.

Augusta, her lovely brow marred by a frown, asked at last, "Why do you wish to meet an earl, cousin?"

"To marry him, of course," said Pen promptly. "Aunt Jane said I must do my best to find a husband so I may not be a charge on you. It simply occurred to me that if I were going to marry, I should do my best to select a husband of some means and stature."

"My dear child!" breathed Mrs. Kendrick, aghast. "You cannot mean to say such things!"

"But why not?" asked Pen reasonably. "Aunt Jane told me many times that it is the custom for young ladies to make their curtsies each year with the intention of securing an advantageous match."

"Yes, dear, I know, but . . ." Further words failed Mrs. Kendrick, and she found herself feeling altogether bewildered. She knew that her granddaughter had spoken nothing save the truth. And it was equally true that every young woman of society embarked upon a London season with the hope of securing the attentions of the most eligible of men. But there seemed to be, in Mrs. Kendrick's opinion, a certain amount of frank naiveté in Penelope's words that was oddly discomfiting.

"I do not believe," she said at last, in a disapproving tone, "that you need worry yourself over such things. You are far too young to be concerned with marriage."

"I am nineteen," said Pen reasonably, "and on more than one occasion Aunt Jane has given her head a shake and told me I am virtually on the shelf. She said that if I do not secure a match very soon I shall end my days a spinster, just like her."

Augusta emitted an odd, choking sound that prompted Mrs. Kendrick to say, rather rigidly, "Your cousin Augusta is nineteen years, and I, for one, would not consider that she is at all on the shelf, my dear!"

Pen looked swiftly up into Augusta's beautiful face, but was hard put to tell from her expression if Augusta was amused or distressed by her words. She said, most sincerely, "I hope I didn't offend you. Indeed, that was not my intention at all. I was only repeating what dear Aunt Jane told me, and it has been my experience that she was usually right about such things."

For the first time in a good many years Mrs. Kendrick found herself at a loss for words. She also felt the suspicion of a violent headache coming on—the result, no doubt, of being dealt too many things to think about at one time. She had no pretensions toward cleverness, and usually was quite willing to succumb to a will stronger than her own. She was, therefore, no match for the frank, engaging young woman who sat beside her with bright-eyed expectancy.

Of a certain, Penelope was right, she realized. Every

unattached young woman who entered society did so for the express purpose of contracting a suitable alliance. Hadn't Mrs. Kendrick launched beautiful Augusta just last year with the very same expectation in mind? Such intentions, however, though prevalent, simply were not discussed.

She eyed Pen warily. "My dear, are you not tired after your journey? I should perhaps warn you that we keep rather late hours here at Rosemount. No doubt you'll wish to rest before supper is announced." She stood and began to move toward the bellpull, saying, "I'll have you shown to your room now, my dear, so you may have plenty of time to rest before supper."

Augusta rose, too. "No, Grandmama, let me. I'll show Penelope to her room."

Mrs. Kendrick had no objections and Augusta, glad for a chance to be alone with Pen, led the way up the great staircase. Since the moment Pen had arrived, her cheeks glowing and her voice tinged with happy enthusiasm, Augusta had found herself drawn to Pen. In her cousin Penelope she thought she detected a genuineness and a certain amount of innocence that she had never before encountered in any other young woman of her acquaintance. She was quickly fairly well convinced that her impression was correct. No sooner did they enter Pen's bedchamber and the door was closed behind them than Pen swept quickly about the room, clasped her hands together, and said most appreciatively, "What a lovely room! I know I shall like it here, very much. I have never before stayed in a house as grand as Rosemount."

"I'm glad you like it," said Augusta politely.

"I rather think it is perfect, just like you."

"Like . . . like *me?*" repeated Augusta, with a slight laugh.

"Of course! I thought so the very moment I arrived and saw you and Grandmama in the salon. You looked so perfect, you see. And I thought how happy each of you must be."

Augusta laughed again, but this time her laughter sounded a bit hollow. "I suppose looks can be deceiving," she said.

"Are you telling me you are *not* happy? But how can that be when you have so much? Surely, handsome looks and wealth and the excellence of a distinguished family name bring you happiness."

"You will find, cousin, that the things you just mentioned bring little happiness at all. One cannot trade upon handsome looks, you know, and wealth cannot be spent if it is controlled by another."

Pen looked at her keenly, thinking that Augusta's words, while not exactly bitter, were impassioned enough to cause her to think that they sprang more from a specific injury than a general unhappiness. She asked, "Indeed? Then tell me, who controls *your* wealth?"

"Our cousin, Owen. You will find that Owen Kendrick controls *everything.*"

"And who is Cousin Owen? I am certain I have never heard Aunt Jane mention him."

"That is because he is not precisely our cousin, but is related to us by marriage only. Owen's father married our grandmama. It was a second marriage for both of them, and they were quite happy. Even Owen seemed glad of the marriage, but when his father passed away Owen became quite odious and hateful. He begrudges all of us the least pleasure, and he keeps poor Grandmama dependent upon him for every shilling.''

Pen's expressive brown eyes swept over the richly appointed bedchamber, with its draperies of rose silk at the windows and costly brocades hanging from the bed canopy. Through the window, she could see the carefully tended flower gardens stretching out from the house and the expanse of neatly manicured lawns that carpeted the rolling hills beyond. Certainly, to Pen's way of thinking, the Kendrick family did not appear to be living in poverty. Nor did it seem that Mr. Owen Kendrick, if he was indeed in charge of the family purse strings, could be accused of stinting on any of the finer things in life.

She gave her slim shoulders a slight shrug and said with a lack of concern, "I hope our Cousin Owen will not begrudge a shilling to me, for I haven't any of my own, you know. I'm quite done in at the heels. When my mama and papa died, they left me with no inheritance and no dowry of any kind. Had it not been for Aunt Jane's kindness in taking me in when I was a child, who knows where I should have found a home?''

Augusta stared at her a moment, her lovely features marred by an expression of shock mixed with concern. "Tell me, Cousin Penelope, do you always speak so openly?''

"Certainly. I have no reason to speak other than

the truth," said Pen simply as she examined with interest the various bottles and jars arrayed across the top of the dressing table.

"Oh, I didn't mean to imply that you speak anything less than the truth," Augusta swiftly assured her. "It is only that . . . cousin, most people do not speak of the same topics you seem to speak on."

Pen looked up quickly. "But what have I said?"

"You mentioned money, for one, and you admitted to being done in at the heels. You might as well know that Grandmama would have swooned to hear such cant coming from a young lady."

"Would she? Then I must be careful in future. Tell me, what other things have I said that I shouldn't have?"

Augusta sat down on the edge of the bed. "Well, I believe Grandmama was a bit taken aback by your speaking so candidly about marrying a peer."

"Was she? Now I *am* surprised, for I was hoping I might be able to rely upon her to help in my search for a suitable husband."

Augusta eyed her appraisingly. "You *are* very frank!"

Pen looked up then and saw Augusta's expression of confused concern. "Have I said something wrong again? Please tell me if I have upset you!"

"No, no! You haven't upset me, although I dare not consider what Grandmama would think if she were to hear you speak so. Of course, it doesn't bother me that you say such things. It is only that . . . your manner of speech is very . . . ." She paused a moment, then said with conviction, "No young lady of my acquaintance would ever say such things."

"They wouldn't?"

"No, and they don't announce in drawing rooms that they are searching for husbands."

"Are you saying I should *not* wish to be married?" asked Pen in a puzzled tone.

"Oh, no! Of course you must be married. Every young lady should be. We just don't speak of it, that's all."

"I see. Then I do not suppose it would be a very good notion to ask our Cousin Owen to inquire among his circle of friends to see if I might find a suitable match in that quarter?"

Augusta laughed slightly, saying, "No, cousin, I rather think that is one notion you should let go by."

"Do you think Cousin Owen would be more inclined to help me search for a husband among his friends if I were to explain my situation? Perhaps if I told him that I have no money of my own and no skill or talent by which to earn a living, he will take pity on me."

"I cannot imagine Owen taking pity on anyone," said Augusta, bitterly. "A more selfish and tightfisted man you will never meet!"

These impassioned words came to the fore of Pen's mind later that evening, long after Augusta had left her to dress for dinner. Pen took extra care with her appearance, and hoped she would be found worthy of keeping company with her elegant and fashionable relatives. She could not imagine Augusta capable of telling falsehoods, yet—as she descended the grand staircase and made her way down the hall toward the yellow drawing room where everyone was to gather before dinner—Pen could not imagine that the family was in as straightened circumstances as Augusta had described. Everywhere Pen looked she saw riches. From garden-cut flower arrangements arrayed in jeweled vases to looking glasses hung with gold gilt frames, it appeared to Pen that the Kendrick family was quite plump in the pockets.

A footman threw open the doors of the drawing room, and Pen entered to find the room empty save for one lone occupant.

A gentleman was seated near the fire, idly glancing through the pages of a periodical. He looked up at the sound of the door closing behind Pen. He was dressed plainly but elegantly in a conservative black coat and pantaloons. His waistcoat was purest white, as was his neckcloth, and amid its folds a single small diamond caught the candlelight and glinted teasingly.

His dark brows rose briefly. Then he stood and held out his hand, saying, "Cousin Penelope? It appears you and I have something in common already—we both are anxious for our supper! It's a pity, but we shall have to wait upon the others, I'm afraid."

His handshake was brief, his smile merely polite, yet Pen, whose habit was to make a quick judgment of any new acquaintance, thought there was something about him that was somehow likable.

He was certainly handsome. His dark hair shone almost blue-black in the reflected light of the candles that illuminated the room, and his eyes, by contrast, were a rather piercing blue. He was tall yet not overly so, and his figure was trim and exuded a quiet strength that made her think he was very used to taking charge of any situation.

He offered her a chair and waited until she was seated before asking politely, "I hope your aunt Jane was well when you left her. Tell me, did you have a comfortable journey?"

"Yes, indeed! In fact, I had a most *adventurous* journey. I intended to tell Grandmama of it as soon as I arrived, but was distracted by the warmth of her welcome. Cousin Owen, you shall be astonished when I tell you of the adventure I had!"

"I'm sure I shall be," he said politely, "but I rather think your grandmother would like to hear your story, too. Perhaps you should wait until she joins us before you tell it."

As Mrs. Kendrick entered the room at that moment with Augusta close upon her heels, Pen did not have long to wait. The family settled together in chairs drawn close by the fire while a footman served sherry to Mrs. Kendrick and Owen, and punch to Pen and Augusta.

Owen asked politely after the health and well-being of each of the ladies until a short lull in the conversation convinced Pen that the time had come to tell them about her encounter with the highwayman. But no sooner did she form the resolve to do just so than the door to the drawing room flew open and a man burst into the room.

He was a young man of perfect visage. In his flawless

features Pen saw an immediate similarity to Augusta; they shared the same acquiline nose, the same strong but pleasing chin, and the same blue eyes framed by dark lashes. His clothes were a veritable patterncard of the *beau monde*, from the points of his starched shirt collar to the tips of his polished boots. Pen had never before seen a man of such fashion, and she was most dutifully impressed.

He was, by all standards, a handsome man, but on this occasion his face was suffused with angry color and his manner was agitated in the extreme. In his fist he held a paper, which he waved aloft in Owen's general direction. He exclaimed in a voice of deep injury, "Never have I been the victim of such dastardly behavior! I demand an explanation for this!"

"Peter, dear, what is it?" asked Augusta, much alarmed. "What has made you so angry?"

"Treachery!" answered the young man, his angry gaze never wavering from Owen's face. "I have borne all the slights and wounds I intend to bear from you, Owen Kendrick! Why, were it not for my grandmother and her affection for you I should send my second to wait upon you!"

In the face of this impassioned speech, Owen Kendrick looked upon the young man with emotionless blue eyes. "Peter, you forget your manners. You have not yet made the acquaintance of your cousin, I think. Allow me to introduce you to Miss Penelope Hamilton. Cousin Penelope, this fellow is Augusta's brother."

The young man stopped short, unsure of what to do next. Certainly, Owen's cool reminder had taken a good deal of the angry wind from the young man's sails, and good manners dictated that he acknowledge the introduction. He flushed slightly, and after a moment he made a stiff bow in Pen's direction and said with immense dignity, "Peter Berwick . . . your servant!"

He gave Pen no opportunity to reply, for he immediately turned back toward Owen, once again waved the paper aloft, and summoned as much of his previous anger as possible.

"Are you or are you not responsible for this?" demanded Peter Berwick. "Did you or did you not cut off my line of credit with my tailor?"

"I did," said Owen quietly.

"By God, do you know what you have done? You've ruined me, that's what!"

Owen took a negligent sip from his glass. "You would naturally think so."

"I could not think otherwise! Only wait until the prince hears of this! I shall be cut, and then you'll see! We shall *all* be ruined!"

"I cannot think how," said Owen. "Surely the prince will be understanding of your predicament. He is, after all, just as foolish and prone to debt as you. The only difference between you and the prince is that you haven't a father who is king to bail you out of your debts. You have, instead, only me."

Peter's face darkened to an angry color. "By God, I shall not stand for this! I shall send a message to you in the morning, Kendrick!"

"Peter, you mustn't say things you cannot mean," said Mrs. Kendrick in a tone that was more nervous than soothing. "I am sure Owen can be made to see reason. Owen, dear, it was cruel of you to cut off Peter's credit with his tailor. Only think how much we rely upon dear Peter to look smart and advance our social standing. Why, his friendship with the Prince Regent alone is worth several new coats and any number of waistcoats, I should think."

"Then Peter must say so to his tailor and hope he will accept such nonsense as payment in full. Otherwise, his credit remains closed." Owen poured out a glass of sherry and offered it to Peter. "If you wish to continue this conversation, Peter, I am, of course, willing to do so. However, I recommend that we conduct further discussions in private, like gentlemen. I cannot think your finances are a fitting topic to argue before the ladies."

For a long moment, Peter weighed the prudence of taking Owen's suggestion over the more fulfilling prospect of giving further vent to his outrage. At last he crumpled the offending letter into a ball and threw it with precision into the fire in the hearth. Stiffly, he accepted the glass of sherry, which he downed in a single, swift motion. He then helped himself to a second glass and retreated to the windows at the far side of the room, muttering, "I cannot think what the prince shall say if he should hear of this!"

An uncomfortable silence lingered until Pen touched Mrs. Kendrick's hand to draw her attention and asked, "Tell me, ma'am, is my cousin Peter truly acquainted with the regent?"

"Oh, dear me, yes! And while I wouldn't go so far as to say they were intimates, I would be less than truthful if I said they were not constantly in each other's company."

"My brother, Peter, is too modest to tell you so himself," added Augusta, "but he and the prince are almost inseparable. Why, the prince intends to follow Peter here to Brighton. We expect him any day to take up residence at The Pavilion."

Pen's brown eyes widened. "The Pavilion? I beg your pardon, but I do not know this pavilion."

"The Marine Pavilion," said Mrs. Kendrick rather importantly, "is the prince's home. Surely you've heard of it. I daresay we shall be invited there again. I have been before, you know! In fact, I should venture to say with assurance that our social obligations shall increase considerably once the prince arrives!"

From the corner of the room, Peter muttered, "You can thank me for that! Were it not for my friendship with Prinny, nothing of import would ever occur in this house! Without the prince, nothing exciting would ever happen!"

"Something exciting happened to me," said Pen, "and it happened just today, as I was traveling here to Rosemount."

Mrs. Kendrick smiled benignly upon her. "My dear child, I cannot imagine what great adventure you might have had on a simple journey to Brighton."

"Tell us what happened, cousin," said Augusta encouragingly.

After a short pause which she hoped would increase

the drama of her tale, Pen obliged Augusta by saying, in a rather breathless voice, "My coach was set upon by a highwayman! And it was the most *thrilling* experience of my life!"

Pen's words produced their desired effect. Gazing about the room, she knew the satisfaction of seeing her grandmother and cousins staring back at her, each with an expression of stunned surprise.

"A . . . a highwayman!" echoed Mrs. Kendrick. "And you never breathed a word of it! My dear, the danger of it all!"

"I don't believe I was ever in any danger. Although the highwayman did have a pistol and a sword, he never brandished either in my direction. In fact, he was quite handsome and terribly charming, and he treated me with the utmost civility. I confess, he was so agreeable that I truly didn't mind being robbed at all!"

Mrs. Kendrick protested feebly, "My dear, I am convinced you cannot mean such a thing!"

"But I do! The highwayman who stopped my carriage was quite gallant, you see, and unlike any man I have ever met. Why, he even spoke in rhyme, and in such an intriguing manner that when he demanded my jewels, I couldn't think of refusing! He wore a mask, so I could not identify him, but I owe him a tremendous debt for providing me the most thrilling moment of my life!"

Mrs. Kendrick stared at her a long moment. "Oh, dear!" she said at last in a faint voice. Then her gaze flew to Owen's face.

He, too, was staring at Pen as if he had turned to

stone, his glass of sherry poised in the midst of its journey toward his lips. As he stood thus, Pen watched his expression change from one of incredulous resentment to blazing anger, and she knew instinctively that his anger was directed solely at her.

Chapter Three

For several moments Owen Kendrick stood stock-still, unable to speak and unable to trust his rampaging emotions. At last he said, in a level voice which still held a note of contempt, "That was quite the most foolish and irresponsible bit of nonsense I have ever heard come from the mouth of a lady! I hope you shall choose your words more carefully in future, cousin!"

Now it was Pen's turn to be surprised. She had never before encountered such anger, and the realization that it was directed at her was so unnerving as to cause her heart to skip a bit faster. She managed, however, to put up her chin and say bravely, "I cannot guess what I might have said to make you so angry, Cousin Owen."

"Then I shall explain it to you. None but an utterly

foolish girl would consider idolizing a common thief!''

"I'm not foolish, and he wasn't common!'' said Pen, rising quickly to her feet. "I told you, he was a gentleman and he was quite clever. He only robbed me for the noblest of purposes . . . he told me so himself! Why, I should be happy to make his acquaintance again under more pleasing circumstances!''

"You have a very distorted notion of what constitutes a gentleman!'' retorted Owen in a voice of raw control. "Let me assure you that the highwayman who accosted you was no gentleman, and I shall thank you to refrain from spinning romantic nonsense over a man who is not only a thief, but a murderer as well.''

"A murderer?'' Pen gasped in disbelief. "That's . . . that's impossible!''

"You deceive yourself. The man is a common thief and a cold-blooded murderer. He would just as willingly take a life as spare one.''

Pen listened to these words with gathering indignation. Surely, Owen was wrong about the highwayman; surely he was speaking of some other road bandit than the one who had stopped Pen's coach. From the moment she had looked up into the eyes of that dashing brigand, Pen had convinced herself that he was no ordinary man. By the time he had touched his lips to hers, she had begun to think herself most certainly infatuated with him and perhaps even a little bit in love. She had thought of little else but the highwayman since their encounter. How, she wondered, could a man be guilty of such crimes as Owen described and still be capable of kissing her with such tenderness? There had been something dashing and romantic about him that had convinced her in her heart of hearts that he was no mere highwayman. For a moment she doubted that she and Owen were talking about the same man.

She could not, however, doubt Owen's anger. His mouth was clamped into a thin line of control, and his dark brows were drawn together above blue eyes that glared relentlessly at her.

"You are wrong, cousin!" she said fiercely, in a vain attempt to defend her highwayman. "The man who halted my carriage on the road was nothing like the man you have described. I am sure you are speaking of someone else!"

"There is no one else. No other bandit but The Black Bard would have the cheek to torment in such a manner the innocent travelers and the good citizens of this area."

"The Black Bard?" repeated Pen, her attention arrested. "Is that his name? He must be called so, because he dresses in black and speaks in rhyme. Of course! How clever!"

"Of all the foolish—" Owen stopped himself with an effort and set his glass of sherry down on a nearby table with a snap. A dull color crept across his face and his manner was stiff as he looked at Mrs. Kendrick and said in a constricted voice, "You'll forgive me, madam, if I excuse myself from your supper table. I've lost my appetite."

He left the room in an instant; the door was closed behind him. An uncomfortable silence lingered until

Augusta said rather tentatively, "I have seen Owen angry before, but I don't believe I've ever seen him quite as furious as he was just now!"

Peter left his place by the windows to move closer, the better to gain Pen's measure and examine her still flushing countenance. "That's because little Penelope stood up to him! What pluck! No one ever stands up to Owen, and I'm glad I was here to witness it!"

"Peter, dearest, please don't say such things," implored Mrs. Kendrick, bringing a fluttering hand to her forehead. "This has all been very disturbing."

"I didn't mean to disturb you, Grandmama," said Pen, "and I didn't mean to have pluck. I only wished Cousin Owen to realize that his accusations were quite unfounded."

"You shall have to apologize to Owen," said Mrs. Kendrick. "You'll have to find him and—" She broke off as her blue eyes met Pen's fiery, brown ones.

"Never! I shall never apologize, Grandmama! Why, when I think of the injustice of his accusations, I could cry from vexation!"

"But you didn't cry," Augusta pointed out. "You answered him back, kind for kind."

"How could I do otherwise? I simply could not stand by and allow him to accuse The Black Bard of such a crime as murder! It simply isn't true! I know it isn't!"

"*How* do you know?" asked Augusta, sensing that there was more to Pen's story than she had yet heard. "How can you be so sure?"

Pen would have been hard-pressed to answer that

question, but she was saved the trouble of having to do so by the announcement of supper being served. The family moved into the dining room and took their places at the table, but no one seemed inclined to enjoy the meal. They ate in relative silence, and as soon as the last course had been cleared and they had removed to the drawing room, Mrs. Kendrick excused herself with a complaint of the headache and retreated to her room. In a very short while Peter, too, excused himself, leaving Augusta and Pen alone.

While her grandmother and brother had been in the room, Augusta had idly leafed through the pages of the very same periodical Owen had discarded earlier. No sooner did the door close upon them, though, and she found herself alone with Pen, than Augusta abandoned the periodical. "You were very passionate in your defense of your highwayman, cousin! Pray, whatever possessed you to speak to Owen in such a manner?"

"You make it sound as if I did some extraordinary thing. I assure you, I did not!"

"But no one is allowed to argue with Owen. At least, I don't think we are. I know I have never before heard anyone do so, except Peter."

"Then it is high time someone did. He said some very unjust things to me. And I did not at all like hearing him describe me as foolish, for I am not, I assure you!"

"I don't think you're foolish. I think you're very brave. I could never speak to Owen as you did. In fact, I was fearful just watching you."

"Tell me, has our Cousin Owen always been such a tyrant?"

"No, not always. When his father was alive, Owen was quite pleasant and rather affectionate. He used to call me his Little Cousin Gussie, and behaved toward me as an older brother. But when his father died, he changed."

"It is not uncommon, I believe for a person to suffer a change after the death of a loved one," said Pen generously. "Perhaps he is simply still in mourning for his father?"

Augusta gave her golden curls a shake. "It's been two years since Mr. Kendrick passed away. No, I fear the change in Owen is permanent. He has become more like a dictator than an elder brother. He keeps poor Peter on a beggar's allowance, and watches every penny Grandmama spends. And he isn't content merely to manage our money, but insists upon managing our lives, as well! I shall never marry any man of Owen Kendrick's choosing, I assure you!"

As this last pronouncement sounded to Pen like much more of a specific injury rather than a mere generalized complaint, she said, "I do not think any young woman must ever be made to marry a man she cannot like, nor should she be made to select a husband based upon anything more than her affection for him."

Augusta cast her a grateful look. "I knew you would understand! Owen says I am being foolish and romantic, but I feel as you do, Cousin Penelope. To marry a man simply because of his income would be a tragic error!"

"Please, you must call me Pen—Penelope is much too long a name to say with frequency! Now, tell me, who does our Cousin Owen wish you to marry because of his income?"

"No one in particular—not yet, at least! But he has made it very clear that the man I marry must be very wealthy. Last year, when Grandmama went to him to ask him—beg him!—to open up the London town house and provide the funds for a London season, he made it clear that he expected immediate results. He told Grandmama I mustn't entertain any but the most eligible of bachelors, and that Grandmama was to apply to him if she were in doubt about the suitability of any man who showed an interest in me."

"Did he truly say such things? Goodness, it sounds as if he thinks of you more as a commodity to be traded than a cousin to be loved."

"Exactly!" exclaimed Augusta, thinking that Pen had gauged the situation to a nicety. "Owen wanted me to marry a wealthy man, no matter that I may not feel the least affection for him! He relied upon me to find and marry a wealthy husband so as to repair the family fortunes. I couldn't do it, Pen. I simply couldn't do it!"

"You were wise to follow your conscience, cousin," said Pen firmly.

"Neither Grandmama nor Owen thought so, I assure you. I ended my season without having received a single offer. Owen was in a state and Grandmama was a little displeased with me, too. I returned to Rosemount under a cloud of disgrace. If it hadn't been for Robert's kindness and understanding, I would have been utterly miserable.''

"Robert? But who is Robert?" asked Pen, looking quickly at Augusta in time to see a very becoming blush mantle her fair cheeks.

"Robert Carswell is a friend of Owen's. He has a house in town, you know, and he is a very respectable gentleman who has always been kind to me.''

"Has he? He sounds very much like the sort of man one would wish for in a friend.''

"Yes! Yes, he is,'' agreed Augusta as the color in her cheek bloomed a bit more.

Much as she might have liked to, Pen refrained from quizzing her further regarding the admirable Mr. Carswell. She had already been given much to think about for one evening. When she retired for the night a little while later, she was in a reflective mood indeed.

In her bedchamber, Betty was waiting for her. In very little time, Pen was out of her gown and into a nightdress and was seated at the dressing table, idly gazing at her reflection in the mirror as Betty plied a sturdy brush to her curls.

"Betty, when we lived with my aunt Jane we were happy, weren't we?''

"Indeed, we were, miss.''

"Would you say we were poor when we lived with Aunt Jane?''

"It wouldn't be my place to say, miss.''

"But you wouldn't say we were rich, would you?'' persisted Pen.

"If you're going to insist upon an answer, Miss Pen,

I should have to say your aunt provided a comfortable home for you. She didn't have much to give you, but she made sure you were happy."

"That's exactly what I was thinking," said Pen, emphatically. "Isn't it curious that my aunt Jane could live such a contented life with a very modest income, while my grandmother and cousins should be so unhappy when it is evident they are wealthy in the extreme?"

"Now, Miss Pen," said Betty in a warning tone, "don't you go jumping to judgment!"

"I never would," Pen assured her, "but in my defense you should know that I have been at Rosemount less than a day and already I have seen the family squabble twice. I think they must care for each other, else why would they remain in each other's company? Yet something has caused their unhappiness. I wonder if there isn't something I may do to help them."

The brush paused in Betty's hand a moment. "I think, miss, it's sometimes best to let people work out their own difficulties, if you understand my meaning."

"Perhaps, but I can't help thinking there might be something I can do," said Pen as she climbed into bed and pulled the covers up beneath her chin.

Having known nothing but happiness and affection from a doting aunt, Pen had assumed quite blithely that all her family members were equally happy in their lives. It had never occurred to her that they might be otherwise, but she now knew that she had stepped into the center of a very unhappy household.

Her aunt Jane had often told Pen that she was kindhearted to a fault, and had hinted on more than one occasion that Pen's desire to right the woes of everyone around her would one day be her undoing. Pen Hamilton did not agree. She didn't think that any harm could ever come from trying to help other people—and the Kendrick family, she decided, was in dire need of help.

From affection sprang the determination to change their circumstance, and she went to bed with that resolve foremost in her mind. In the morning she awoke to find that her resolution had not weakened, but neither had her mind hit upon a plan to steer her grandmother and cousins from the unhappy course they were traveling.

Pen's grandmother had warned her that meals at Rosemount were served late; breakfast, she discovered, was no exception.

Betty entered her room bearing a cup of cool milk and a slab of bread with cheese, saying, "There's no food to be had at this hour, no breakfast covers laid, and not even a fire in the kitchens yet. I brought what I could, miss. It's not much, but it will have to do until the household is roused from their beds."

As her empty stomach had already begun to grumble, Pen accepted the meager meal gratefully. She had no notion what hour of the day her grandmother usually left her chamber, and she itched for activity. With Betty's help, Pen donned her riding kit and went off in search of the stables.

She entered to find an elderly groom plying a currycomb to a gleaming horse. He looked up at her approach, offered a curt nod, and went back to his work.

"Good morning!" said Pen cheerfully. "That's a beautiful animal. Has he been out yet this morning?"

The groom looked up without pausing in his work and eyed Pen appraisingly. "Yes, miss. He's just come in from his morning run."

"I wish I had been here to see it. He's a jumper, isn't he?"

The groom paused then and regarded Pen again, but this time there was a faint expression of astonishment in his eyes. "Yes, miss. How did you know?"

"He has a little scar just above the coronet of his right front leg. He must have scraped it at one time as he went over a fence or rock wall."

The groom rubbed a thoughtful hand over his unshaven chin. "Yes, miss, he did indeed. You know your horses, I'm thinking."

"I'm very fond of all animals," she replied, smiling. The groom resumed his work and Pen stood in silence, surveying with interest the many horses in their various stalls before returning her attention to the groom. "You have a very fine stable here."

"That would be Master Owen's doing. He has an excellent eye, I think."

"Master Owen?" she repeated. "Why, you must have known him when he was much younger, to call him that."

"Yes, miss. It's old habit that makes me address him so. I worked for his father, you see, and came to know Master Owen when he was naught but a lad.

I taught him to ride and to dress his mount when he was just out of leading strings.''

"He's my cousin, you know. My name is Miss Penelope Hamilton."

"Yes, miss," said the groom without looking up.

"What shall I call you?"

He stopped then, and gave her his full regard. "I'm Tom Hawkins, miss."

"Well, then, Tom Hawkins, do you think you might find a suitable mount for me?"

"I could indeed, miss. Master Owen has already selected a horse for you, in case you was wishin' to ride." He led Pen over to a stall in which a very docile mare was quartered.

"This horse?" she asked, disappointed.

"Yes, miss. This here is Phoebe. She's a nice, tame horse for a lady."

"I can see my cousin doesn't think much of my riding ability. To be frank, Tom Hawkins, I was hoping for an animal with a bit more spirit. What about that one over there?" she asked, pointing to the very horse Tom had been brushing since first she had entered the stables.

"Ahh, now, that's the master's hunter. I'm afraid you can't have that one, miss."

"Then what about this one?" she said, having caught sight of a chestnut mare in a nearby stall. The animal raised her head and nervously tamped her feet at Pen's approach.

Pen gently stroked the animal's neck and softly murmured a few words in a comforting tone.

Patiently, she continued to do so until the beautiful animal calmed somewhat.

Tom Hawkins watched as the horse tossed her head coquettishly and then dipped her head back down again, the better for Pen to stroke her nose and murmur endearments into her ear. "You've got a way with horses, I see, Miss."

"I like this one. What's her name?"

"Little Angel."

Pen laughed. "What an odd name, indeed! Tell me, is she truly angelic?"

"Most of the time she's as good as they come, and a sweet goer, too. If it's a gallop you want, she can give you a ride that could rival any derby winner's. But she's got a bag of tricks, this one. The only trouble is, you never know when she's going to dip into that bag and pull out a bit of mischief."

"She sounds marvelous! Please, may I ride her? I promise I shall take extra care with her, and I shall have her back to you in good order."

Tom shook his head. "No, miss. I'm afraid our Little Angel is a bit too unpredictable for someone as little as you. If she was to take one of her fancies into her head, you'd never hold her. Why, Master Owen would have my hide if I was to saddle you up and send you off, only to have something happen to you."

"But what could possibly happen?"

"It's hard to say, and that, don't you see, is the problem!"

"But I'm an excellent horsewoman, I assure you!"

Tom Hawkins shook his head. "No, miss. I could

never trust Little Angel enough to send you out alone on her!''

"Then come with me," said Pen. "Ride with me for a little way and see for yourself how she fares with me on her back."

Tom rubbed his grizzled chin as he considered the notion. "I suppose you couldn't come to any harm with me nearby."

"Exactly! We'll ride out together, and you'll see!" Pen nuzzled her face against the animal's neck. "Little Angel likes me already, I can tell. She'll be a most well-mannered and perfectly behaved mount. Of that I'm certain."

"That's as may be, but if she takes it into her head to pull up skittish, we'll come straight back to the stables, yes?"

"Of course!" Pen assured him.

Tom gave the matter another moment's thought, then set about saddling Little Angel for Pen and a second horse for himself. In a very short time he threw Pen up on Little Angel's back and patiently waited while she arranged her skirts over the pommel and saddle.

They left the buildings of Rosemount behind at a sedate canter, and Pen was afforded an opportunity to take Little Angel's measure.

They came upon a wide meadow, flanked on either side by rolling hills, and Pen felt the urge to see what her horse could do.

"You promised that Little Angel could gallop like a derby winner, Tom Hawkins. I shall hold you to that promise!" Then, with a yelp and a slight slap against her horse's rump, she set Little Angel galloping down the meadow.

Tom Hawkins followed, and together they created a thunderstorm of galloping hooves, flushing quail from their hiding places and sending squirrels scurrying in their wake.

On Little Angel's back Pen felt alive and exhilarated. She moved in natural unison with the animal, her weight forward, her hands gripping the reins with just the right amount of tension, her knees close upon Little Angel's ribs.

By the time she reined her mount in, Pen's breathing was rapid, her cheeks were flushed, and her eyes were bright with happiness. "Why, Little Angel is a treasure! Did you see how fast she ran? Did you see how much she enjoyed that gallop? How foolish you were to worry over the conduct of this horse, Tom!"

"Now, see here, Miss Hamilton, you've been on that animal's back no longer than a pig's whisper, while I've known her since she was a foal! She's a tricky one, and Master Owen, if he were here, would agree with me."

Pen gave a laugh. "I think you and my Cousin Owen worry too much, Tom. Only see how she is itching to gallop again. You must see if you can keep up with us!"

So saying, Pen dug her heels into Little Angel's ribs. The horse took off at a dead gallop, with Pen shrieking in glee and leaving a swirl of dust behind.

Chapter Four

Owen Kendrick reined in his thoroughbred at the top of the rise and wheeled the animal about. For a few moments he remained there, silent except for an occasional admonishment to his fidgeting horse, enjoying the first warm rays of the June sun upon his back.

In the distance the village rooftops peeked from beneath a canopy of trees; only the bell tower of the church pierced the canopy and reached up toward the deep blue of the sky. Before him, in clusters across the valley, great hundred–year–old oaks spread their huge, gnarled branches, weaving patterns of shade across patches of lush, green lawn.

As a youth Owen had climbed those trees, as had his father before him. In all, four generations of Kendrick men had skinned their elbows and bruised their knees on the great oaks of Rosemount. Owen considered those old trees just as much a part of his heritage as the manor house itself, the artwork that hung in its gallery, or the plate and silver that graced its halls.

He took a deep breath of the cool morning air. It was clear and, to his mind, deliciously sweet after his having tasted the sooty air of London. Business had taken him to the great city, and he had returned to Rosemount only two days before. After the relentless noise of London and its congestion of people and traffic, he appreciated Rosemount even more—its beauty, its serenity, and the warm feeling of security it offered. He always felt at peace when he was at Rosemount, and it pained him whenever he considered just how close he was to losing it.

Out of the corner of his eye, a movement caught his attention. Turning, he saw two riders on horseback racing through the east meadow. He recognized Tom Hawkins instantly, for he knew Tom's seat on a horse as well as he knew his own. He did not, however, recognize the other rider, who rode with sufficient skill to outpace Tom by several lengths.

Owen urged his horse forward toward the edge of the rise. The animal minced and shied slightly, but with a determined hand on the rein Owen sent his horse scurrying down the slope.

He drew to a halt at the foot of the hill and heard Penelope Hamilton's voice call out to him. She waved her hand happily in his direction, calling, "Good morning, Cousin Owen! You see we are enjoying an invigorating ride!"

She cantered toward him, with Tom following at a discreet distance behind. As she drew near, Owen saw that her brown eyes were bright with enjoyment, and there was a very becoming flush to her complexion. A few wisps of curly brown hair had come loose from their place beneath her hat and added a certain charm to her appearance.

That charm faded quickly, however, as soon as he recognized the horse on which she sat. "Cousin," he said tersely as he touched his gloved fingers to the brim of his hat. That pleasantry dispensed, he shot a quelling look at his groom. "Tom, this is not the horse I allotted for Miss Hamilton's use during her stay at Rosemount."

"No, it isn't, sir, but I didn't think any harm could come to Miss Hamilton with me riding beside her."

"From what I observed you were not beside her but several lengths behind, and barely able to keep that pace," retorted Owen.

"Please don't scold Tom Hawkins," begged Pen, drawing Owen's attention. "He did tell me I was to ride Phoebe, but I insisted upon this horse instead."

"Little Angel is not a suitable mount for a young lady."

"But Phoebe is not a suitable mount for a true horsewoman."

"Phoebe is a very docile and very well-mannered animal," insisted Owen.

"She is, indeed! But only think how ridiculous I should feel riding such a horse, knowing very well all the while that I am perfectly capable of galloping faster than she!"

He looked at her a long moment. "I daresay you could."

"Then you won't scold Tom for letting me have my way?"

"No, but I shall scold him for allowing you to have Little Angel. There are any number of other horses in my stable you might have chosen if you didn't wish to ride Phoebe. Tom should have steered you away from Little Angel."

"He tried to, believe me," Pen said ingeniously. She leaned forward to give her horse's neck an encouraging pat and asked, "But how could I ignore Little Angel? She is so affectionate and intelligent that I could hardly wish to ride any but her. You saw how splendid a gallop she gave me!"

"I did." He watched her a moment as she cooed endearments into the horse's ear. Then he turned toward the groom, saying, "I'll see Miss Hamilton back to the house, Tom."

Pen cast Owen a sunny smile. "Where shall we ride now? I should like to see more of Rosemount, if you please."

"It shall be my pleasure to show you the rest of the grounds, Cousin Penelope," he said courteously.

"Please, won't you call me Pen? Penelope is a horrid mouthful, and whenever anyone calls me Miss Hamilton I immediately think they are speaking to my aunt Jane, rather than to me."

"As you wish." He said no more, but spurred his horse forward to climb back up one of the rolling hills from which he had earlier surveyed the valley. Pen urged Little Angel to follow. Upon reaching the crest, she watched as Owen's horse caricoled dangerously. The animal's antics lasted only a moment, for he controlled it with an assurance that immediately drew Pen's admiration.

She inspected his thoroughbred with a knowledgeable eye. It was, indeed, a beautiful animal, standing just over fifteen hands with a small head atop an elegantly arched neck. Its chest was broad and its quarters powerful. As if aware of its own strength and grace, the horse stamped at the ground, impatient to be off, and Pen had a sudden notion that the animal was not unlike its master.

She looked up to find Owen's blue eyes upon her, one dark brow cocked questioningly. "Don't tell me you wish to ride this horse, too, Cousin. I would have to disappoint you . . . no one rides Pharaoh but me."

"I could never ride such a horse," she said, with a slight laugh and a shake of her head. "He's quite imposing and I assure you that horses do not usually intimidate me."

"I thought as much."

"Although I must admit, he is not at all the sort of horse I would have pictured as yours. I'm really quite impressed with you now that I've seen you on Pharaoh. Any man who can control such a magnificently spirited animal cannot be quite as conservative and stuffy as you would have everyone believe."

Owen drew his horse to a sudden stop, his blue eyes fixed upon her in astonishment. "That was a rather remarkable thing to say! Tell me, should I be flattered or offended by such a confidence?"

"Flattered, of course. I suppose I should not say so, but sometimes first impressions of persons are not always the correct impression. Take yourself, for example.''

"I should rather not.''

"I'm only trying to make the point that, like everyone else I have met since my arrival at Rosemount, you are not as you first seem.''

He was quiet a moment, and he frowned slightly as his blue eyes examined Pen's face. She thought she saw a change, however subtle, come over him. His back, she thought, had gone a little straighter, and his chin, already of a strong, square cut, had gone a bit more rigid. After a while he said, in a voice void of expression, "Indeed.''

Pen suffered an odd feeling she had committed some horrid offense. "Are you angry with me? Have I said something wrong again, as I did last evening?''

He looked away from her then and said, "Last evening I said some things to you, cousin, that I shouldn't have said. I allowed my temper to reign, and I was wrong. I hope you'll accept my apology.''

She cast him an appraising look. "That was very nicely said. Tell me, are you truly sorry, or are you merely hoping to make peace between us?''

"Don't mistake me, cousin. I am apologizing for my behavior, not for my sentiments.''

"I see,'' she said as she made a great show of examining the pleated fittings on her riding gloves. "Have we, then, agreed to disagree on the subject of The Black Bard?''

"I think we would be better served to agree never to mention him again.''

At first she didn't think she wanted to agree to any

such thing. Owen was wrong about The Black Bard, she told herself. She would dearly love to convince him of such, but there was a granite set to his chin and a tightness about his lips that told her that any argument she might put forth was not likely to alter his opinion. Besides, what argument could she offer up? How could she tell Owen Kendrick that she knew the highwayman's character merely by the way his kiss had felt upon her lips? Or that she knew him to be honorable because of the tender manner with which he had brushed his fingers against her chin?

"Very well," she said at last, "we shall agree not to discuss The Black Bard. But you must know that my opinion of him has not altered in the least."

"I could have guessed as much. Someday perhaps you will tell me what he may have done to incite such blind devotion. In the meantime, perhaps we can hit upon a more neutral topic. Tell me, what made your aunt decide to send you to live with your grandmother at Rosemount?"

"It was not a sudden decision, I think. She has been planning my entrance into society since the day I achieved my eighteenth birthday. She wishes me to gain some polish, and perhaps even have a London season. She is hopeful that under Grandmama's chaperonage I shall contract a brilliant alliance."

He looked at her sharply. "Indeed?"

"Being a spinster herself, Aunt Jane thought she was not the best person to put me in the way of securing a husband, and since Grandmama has had *two* husbands, she would be a better source for finding a match for me."

"I see," he said again, and the line of his jaw hardened.

"*Now* have I said something wrong?" she asked as Owen reined in his horse suddenly.

Not wrong, he thought, *but certainly illuminating.* So, Miss Penelope Hamilton had come to Rosemount to secure for herself a social life, and even aspired to the lofty heights of a London season! Oh, he knew very well that such was the dream of virtually every young woman of marriageable age, but for some reason he was a trifle disappointed. He had noticed something about Pen Hamilton—something guileless and a little naive—that had made him think for just a moment that she might be different than all the other relatives who came to him with their pockets empty and their hands out. To realize that she was no different was somehow discomfiting, and that realization took him a little by surprise.

He said, "Not at all," but that telltale muscle pulsed in his chin and he frowned slightly beneath the brim of his hat. "I think it best we ride back to the stables. I've some estate business to see to this morning. I hope you don't mind?"

She did mind. In fact, she longed for another gallop on Little Angel's back, but the tenuous truce she had struck with Owen prevented her from saying so. They rode back to the stables side by side and arrived to find Tom Hawkins waiting for them. Owen assisted her down and stood by as she gave Little Angel's nose a rub. "She is a wonderful horse," she said. "May I ride her every day?"

"If you like. However, I hope you will take my advice and select a different horse."

A sudden memory of Augusta, lamenting Owen's control over the family, ran through Pen's mind. She was beginning to think that Augusta was right, that Owen did indeed rule over the family in all matters, and she was determined that he should not rule over her.

She set her chin at a mulish angle. "I think I shall ride Little Angel again tomorrow. We get along very well, I think."

He nodded curtly. "As you wish, cousin."

Feeling as if she had won one small victory, Pen returned to the house and changed her dress before presenting herself in the family dining room. Augusta was there before her, finishing the last of her breakfast.

"There you are at last!" she said as Pen took a seat at the table and allowed a footman to place a plateful of food before her. "I have been wondering how long you planned to lay abed today."

"But I've been up for hours. In fact, I just returned from riding out with Owen."

Augusta had been about to pop a bite of toast into her mouth, but at this her hand stopped in mid-air and she looked curiously over at Pen. "Have you? With Owen?"

"Yes indeed, and I could not have enjoyed it more. He's an excellent horseman, and I told him so, of course. I always think it a good idea to let a person know when you admire something about them. Don't you agree?"

"I suppose, but after the spat you had with him last night I didn't think you would find anything to admire about him."

"There you are wrong," said Pen emphatically. "Merely because we had a disagreement does not mean I cannot judge him impartially. In fact, I would venture to say—while I cannot claim to know him very well!—there is enough about him that I do like to make me think that we shall deal very well together."

"Then you have the advantage over me, for I shall never deal well with Owen," said Augusta with a rather mulish set to her chin.

Through the dining room door came Mrs. Kendrick, carrying Candace in the crook of one arm and a clutch of letters in her other hand. "Good morning, Augusta, Penelope!" She took a seat at the table, and no sooner had she settled herself most comfortably than Candace leapt down from her lap and approached Pen's chair.

"Good morning, Grandmama," she said, and she felt an unaccustomed weight upon her legs as the dog jumped into her lap. "Well, good morning, Candace! I hope you are not begging for my breakfast, for I must warn you that I intend to eat every morsel put before me."

"My dear, I hope our breakfast hour is not too late for you," said Mrs. Kendrick with a frown. "You'll find your cousins and I cannot tolerate the sight of food early in the day, and have become accustomed to enjoying a late breakfast."

"I admit I was very hungry, but I was able to occupy

myself this morning. I was just telling Augusta that I had a very enjoyable ride with Cousin Owen.''

"Did you? How curious. I had no notion the man was up and about this morning."

"I believe he rides early every day, Grandmama."

"Does he, indeed? I cannot think why he would wish to. I do not believe there is any point in forcing oneself into strenuous tasks first thing in the day. I much prefer to spend my mornings in less arduous pursuits.''

"I think that's very wise of you," said Pen in what she hoped was a diplomatic tone.

Augusta smiled slightly, but chose to change the subject, saying, "Grandmama has brought the post. Tell us, is there anything of interest this morning?''

"There is, indeed, and you shall never guess the invitations we have received!" Mrs. Kendrick answered happily. "There is to be a very cunning masquerade in a few weeks time. My dear friend Lady Ambersleigh has sent a note round announcing it. And then there is to be a card party with supper at the home of Lord and Lady Belmore. Of course, when the prince arrives in town, there shall be any number of balls and parties to attend.''

Pen's interest quickened. "Grandmama, do you think there is any chance I may meet the prince? Tell me truly, for I should like it above all things!''

"I do not see why you should not, my dear. If the prince comes to Brighton—which is a virtual certainty, you know—he shall keep company with Peter, you may depend upon it. And Peter, bless him, will ensure the family falls under the prince's notice.

"My child, if only you had been with us when Mr. Kendrick was alive," said her grandmother as a light in her eyes kindled at the memory. "Such circles we moved in then! There was a time, you know, when the Kendricks and the Hamiltons were the first families of Brighton. And I don't mind telling you that we piped a pretty fair tune to which everyone in London danced, as well. The balls, the parties! We filled the ballroom in the east wing—I never saw such a crush of people!" Her expression of happiness faded with the memory as she said, "Of course, all that has changed now."

"But what has changed, Grandmama? You still have your family, and Rosemount is still as fine an estate as it ever was. What has changed?"

"Everything, it would seem. We are not invited out much now."

"Whyever not?"

"My dear, I fear we are not invited because we cannot return the invitation," said Mrs. Kendrick sadly.

Seeing the look of confusion on Pen's face, Augusta said rather bitterly, "Owen has forbidden any entertainments at Rosemount. I told you he controls everything!"

"And it is a dreadful shame," lamented Mrs. Kendrick. "The most magnificent balls were held in this very house, and we would sit forty to dine in the long gallery! Sadly, those days are gone. We shall never see the likes again."

"Why not, Grandmama?" asked Pen. "Rosemount

is a magnificent estate. Why do you not have a ball or a party of your own?"

Mrs. Kendrick did not answer immediately, but dabbed at her suddenly misting eyes with the corner of her table napkin.

Augusta watched her with an empathetic eye and said softly, "Owen has closed the east wing of Rosemount where the gallery and the ballroom are located. *He* said it was because that part of the house is damaged from neglect, but *I* know he merely wishes to forbid us any entertainment at all."

"That does not sound like something Owen would do," Pen said thoughtfully.

"You don't know him as well as we," Augusta reminded her. "I assure you, he is capable of even worse behavior!"

"My dears, there is no good to come of fretting over something we cannot change," Mrs. Kendrick said, as she dried her tears and gave a ladylike sniff.

"I told you that Owen controls everything," Augusta reminded Pen. "I cannot even have a new reticule without his permission. I have needed a new driving coat for the longest time, and even that is denied me."

Pen gave her head a small shake. "You make him sound like an ogre!"

"He is not, of course," said Mrs. Kendrick, "for in his own way Owen is a very thoughtful man and very smart, too, which makes me think there must be some reason for him to behave the way he does from time to time."

Pen cast her a worried look. "Do you think he will

allow us to attend the parties and assemblies you mentioned? Must we decline the invitations we received?"

"It would be just like Owen," said Augusta pessimistically, "to forbid us the treat of attending any parties at all."

Mrs. Kendrick drew herself up, and said in a voice stronger than before, "Nonsense! He would never do such a thing. If he does—and I doubt he will—I shall insist he reconsider!"

"Would you, Grandmama?" asked Augusta, clearly doubtful.

"Certainly! I shall be the first to admit that Owen has been allowed to have his own way, but on a subject as important as attending neighborhood entertainments I shall have to insist that he stand aside. This is too crucial a time in your lives, my dear girls. You must be seen at all the right parties and routs. You must be beautifully coiffed and gowned at all times. Penelope, my dear, we must ensure you have an acceptable ball gown. If you do not, we must go shopping first thing today."

Augusta gasped. "Grandmama! You know we must not! What would Owen say if we were to indulge in such extravagance?"

"He would say that we are justified, I am sure! Owen cannot expect his dear cousin to attend any assemblies dressed in country rags. I shall apply to him. I am sure Owen shall agree with me!"

"Agree with you about what?" asked that very gentleman as he entered the room with Peter one step behind him.

Mrs. Kendrick hesitated a moment as both men claimed seats at the table. She would very much liked to have petitioned her case before her nephew in privacy, just in case he took exception to her request, but she had spoken with such bravado only a moment before that she couldn't back down now. Straightening her shoulders a little, she said, "Your little cousin, Penelope—do you not think she should be properly gowned before she ventures out to any parties in the neighborhood?"

"Most certainly," said Owen in an even tone that did nothing to encourage her.

"Then I should like to take her into Brighton for a bit of shopping. She shall need a ball gown, Owen."

He looked up then, his expression unreadable, but his gaze settled upon Pen and remained there for a moment or two. Under his scrutiny, she felt a gentle flush of heat rise in her face and she felt, of a sudden, unaccountably shy.

A footman placed a cup of coffee before Owen and he took a slow sip before he replied. "Yes, she shall. You are correct, as usual, madam."

Without realizing it, Mrs. Kendrick had been holding her breath, awaiting Owen's reply. At this she let out a deep sigh and gave a short laugh of surprise. "Thank you, my dear! Thank you, indeed! We shall see to the arrangements today, I think. Augusta, you must come along, too, for an outing into Town shall do you good. Yes, indeed, this is all most splendid!"

"No, it isn't!" interjected Peter in a rising voice. "It isn't splendid at all! How is it that my credit has been cut off, yet you will finance a new rig for Cousin Penelope?"

"It is hardly the same thing," said Owen calmly.

"Isn't it?" demanded Peter. "In case you have forgotten, cousin, I have a position to maintain—a station to preserve! I have a place in society that requires a certain level of style."

"You also have a mountain of debts that you have neither the intent nor the wherewithal to pay."

Peter shot him a look of cold anger. "Don't speak of my debts unless you mean to pay them," he warned.

"Then we shall not speak of them again," said Owen with perfect calm.

Chapter Five

In the aftermath of such a confrontation, Pen did not think she could enjoy an afternoon of shopping with her grandmother and cousin. The memory of the arguments she had witnessed between Owen and Peter left her feeling uneasy, for the basis of their quarrel was Owen's refusal to pay for Peter's new clothes. It made no sense that Owen should agree instead to pay for hers.

She was unable to shake that feeling of unease as she tied the ribbons of her bonnet beneath her chin and scooped up her gloves, then went downstairs to join her grandmother and cousin. She reached the front hall at the very same moment the butler opened the front door to admit a visitor to the house.

A young man stepped across the threshold. He swept a tall, curly-brimmed hat from his head and handed it, along with gloves and driving cape, to a nearby footman. He flashed a smile at the butler, saying, "Good day, Beardsley. Tell me, is that rascal Owen Kendrick about?"

The butler, while gratified by such a greeting from a visitor he had often described as a most superior gentleman, maintained his stoic expression. "Mr. Kendrick is, indeed, at home, sir."

"Good, for I've a bone to pick with him. Ask him to join me in the yellow salon, won't you, Beardsley? No need to usher me about—I know my way!"

The gentleman turned then and caught sight of Pen, poised on the bottom step of the stair. A questioning light leapt in his blue eyes and he cocked his blonde head slightly to one side. "Forgive me! I had no notion anyone else was about."

"Nor could you have known, for I just now came down the staircase behind you. I am to meet my grandmother and my cousin here, and then we are on our way out."

"Your grandmother and cousin?" he repeated. "Don't tell me you live here? Well, then, we shall not wait upon formalities and proper introductions, for I am virtually a resident here myself! I am Robert Carswell, a friend of Owen's."

Pen recognized his name immediately. So, this was Mr. Carswell, the very same Mr. Carswell of whom Augusta had spoken the evening before. She looked up into his blue eyes, alight with friendly good humor, and she felt an immediate liking for him. "Tell me, are you truly a friend of my cousin Owen?"

"You sound surprised," he said with a slight smile. "Owen does have friends, I assure you!"

She laughed then, and said, "Forgive me! I didn't mean to sound surprised; it is only that Owen is so . . . so—"

"Yes, he is, isn't he?" said Mr. Carswell, sympathetically. "He *will* act the lord of the manor, whether anyone wants him to or not. I think he has taken it into his head that a man of his responsibilities must be sober and levelheaded at all times."

"And is he?"

"Not when I have anything to say in the matter. In fact, I'm here to persuade him to come with me into Town. I'm engaged to meet some friends, and I've a notion it would do him good to come along."

"By coincidence, I am engaged to go into Town, as well," said Pen. "I am about to venture there with my grandmother and cousin on a shopping expedition."

His light brows flew skyward. "Your cousin is going shopping? *Owen?*"

"No, no, not Owen," she said, laughing. "My cousin Augusta will accompany Grandmama and me."

"I am relieved!" he said in a teasing tone that charmed her. "For a moment I entertained the notion of Owen Kendrick rummaging through the ribbons and laces of the fabric bazaar and—" He broke off, suddenly seeing Augusta at the top of the stair.

She was dressed quite fetchingly in a spencer of blue grosgrain and a bonnet adorned with ribbons of the same fabric. She began her descent, her cheeks mantled by a faint tinge of color—summoned, no doubt, by the fact that Mr. Carswell was staring up at her with a look of undisguised admiration. By the time she achieved the bottom step, the faint color had bloomed into a full-scale blush, and a shy smile of uncertainty animated her pink lips.

Robert Carswell stepped forward and briefly clasped her hand, saying, "Miss Berwick! A special delight! I had not dared think I might see you! I had hoped, of course—! I mean, I am always glad for an opportunity to speak to you—! How . . . how do you do?"

It was a curious thing, thought Pen, that the same man she had thought so composed and articulate a mere moment before could be reduced to such a stammering quagmire only seconds later. When she happened to notice that Augusta had dissolved into an equally uncertain state, Pen found that her interest in the couple was fairly well caught.

Augusta slowly withdrew her fingers from Mr. Carswell's grasp and said shyly, "It . . . it is a pleasure to see you again, sir. Tell me, have you met my cousin, Pen? Grandmama would want you to be properly introduced."

"We're old friends by now, aren't we, Miss . . . Miss . . . Pen, is it? No, I cannot think that is right!"

"My name is Penelope, sir. Penelope Hamilton, to be exact, but I am known to my family and friends as Pen."

"Fortunate family and friends," he said, with a slight smile that reminded her of his earlier charm.

Mrs. Kendrick joined them, her little white dog nestled in her arms, a bonnet of enormous proportions upon her head, and her shawls trailing behind. "Ah, I see you have met our Mr. Carswell. Augusta, did you perform the introductions? Excellent! I am afraid, however, you shall have to excuse us, Mr. Carswell. We are about to go into Town."

"But Mr. Carswell is bound for Brighton, as well, Grandmama," said Pen impetuously. "Could he not ride along in our carriage?"

Robert Carswell said quickly, "I think not, Miss Hamilton, although I am pleased by your suggestion."

"Won't you reconsider? I am sure there is sufficient room for you. You may sit beside my grandmother, but I fear that means you shall be obliged to spend the entire ride gazing at Augusta and me."

"An obligation I should welcome," he said, casting a soft, lingering look at Augusta.

Under his constant gaze, Augusta Berwick averted her eyes. The blush reappeared to color her cheeks, and her hands, holding kidskin gloves, nervously worked the fingers of the gloves into a deplorable, wrinkled knot.

Watching these effects, Pen couldn't help but wonder over them. It was rather evident to her that Mr. Carswell was quite smitten with Augusta. And she had a fairly good notion that Augusta returned his regard.

Only Mrs. Kendrick seemed oblivious to the silent exchange between them. She said rather haphazardly, "Very prettily said, Mr. Carswell. Of course, you are welcome to join us, if it will make my dear Penelope happy."

"Much as I am tempted by your invitation, I fear I must decline."

Mrs. Kendrick moved off toward the door, saying, "You do as you like. Come along, my dears. There is much to be done today if we are to find a gown for Penelope!"

Pen dipped a curtsy and said good-bye to Robert, then followed her grandmother and Augusta out of the house and into the waiting carriage.

They set off toward Town at a brisk pace. Through the window of the carriage Pen could see the spires of The Marine Pavilion which loomed far above the distant treetops. Mrs. Kendrick described to her the fantastic design of the prince's residence and the wonders of its rooms.

"Grandmama, may we not drive by The Pavilion so Pen may see it?" asked Augusta.

"Not today, I fear. Penelope, my love, you must not be disappointed if we leave that treat for another time. I assure you that when the prince arrives, dear Peter shall secure invitations for us to be invited there as guests. There is no need to think we must drive past The Pavilion as if we were mere gawkers!"

Augusta said with a hint of pride, "Grandmama has been to The Pavilion before, you know. She has seen the prince and The Pavilion in all their finery."

"And you, my dear Penelope, shall need some finery of your own. You must understand that the prince demands beauty in everything about him. Of course, your face and deportment are much to your credit, and I think he shall be pleased with you there, but we must ensure you are properly gowned. My *modiste* shall see to that! She has an excellent eye for these sorts of things, and can be relied upon to produce the perfect frock.''

Penelope soon learned that a dress of such perfection could not be designed in a mere matter of minutes. Their arrival at the dressmaker's shop produced a whirlwind of activity; there were design books to pour over, fabrics to be chosen, trims to be selected. The *modiste*, a rather forbidding woman who ordered her assistants about with military precision, condescended to take Pen's measurements herself. She set about doing so with pins and string, instructing Pen at intervals to raise first one arm, then the other, to stand up straight and to cease fidgeting.

''Well, madame, what say you?'' asked Mrs. Kendrick when the dressmaker at last set her tools aside. ''Have you a design in mind for my granddaughter?''

The *modiste* brought her hands together in a sharp, imperious clap and one of her minions scurried out of the room. She returned a moment later bearing a large bundle wrapped in tissue, which she tenderly spread upon a tabletop.

Madame waved one of her hands slightly, and her minions unwrapped the package to reveal a gown the likes of which Pen had never seen. Its design was of the Greek style, favored by ladies of fashion, and its lines were familiar: a short bodice and straight skirt combined to create a long, column-like silhouette. But in this dress there was an artistry that quite caught Pen's attention. The gown was made of pale, rose-colored muslin, embroidered at the hem with delicate flowers fashioned in white. The skirts were comprised of thin layers of fabric cut full at the back so as to extend to a small train behind. The neckline was low and layered with filmy wisps of fabric that draped elegantly about the shoulders to fall into a graceful spill down the back of the dress. In all, it was an extraordinary gown, and Pen reached out instinctively to reverently finger the delicate fabric.

"Grandmama! Have you ever seen such a dress?" she breathed.

"No, miss, she has not," said the *modiste*, "for there is not another gown like it in all of England. I designed this for a young lady with hair and eyes much the color of yours. For two months we labored over this gown, and by the time it was finished the foolish girl had gained three stone. I forbade her to have it! I have saved it for the right young lady who will do it justice. You are that lady!"

Augusta, looking at the dress with her blue eyes gone wide, said, "It's very daring! Pen, could you bring yourself to wear such a gown?"

Longingly, Pen touched the delicate fabric and trims on the dress. Its workmanship was exquisite, its style extraordinary, yet Pen knew, too, that such artistry did not come without cost. "Yes, I think I could wear it. In fact, I should be proud to do so, but—" She cast a look of worry toward her grandmother and debated the prudence of raising the issue of cost. Instead, she said rather hopefully, "But, perhaps, Grandmama, you may think this dress is too elegant, too sophisticated for a girl such as me."

"Nonsense, my love! This is exactly the sort of gown we were looking for!" Mrs. Kendrick declared.

Still Pen hesitated. "But . . . do you not think the gown is more suited to a lady who is, perhaps, taller?"

"My dearest girl, the dressmakers shall alter the gown to your measurements. Did you think we would send you off to a party tripping over hemlines and trims?" asked Mrs. Kendrick with a laugh.

"No, Grandmama, but—"

"We shall take the gown, madame! I shall trust you to see that it is delivered on time, now!"

Pen waited until they had finished the alterations and left the shop before she asked in a rather small, rather troubled voice, "Grandmama, the gown is beautiful, but I am convinced it must be very dear! Should we not have asked the price before we claimed it?"

"My dearest child, you cannot mean such a thing!" gasped Mrs. Kendrick in alarm. "A lady would never stoop to such behavior as asking the price of a gown! It is unthinkable!"

"But how shall we know for certain we can afford such a purchase?"

"My dear, we do not have to afford it," said Mrs. Kendrick, patiently. "Owen shall settle the reckoning. Now, not another word on the matter! I refuse to haggle over prices on the street like a dairyman's wife!"

Pen was fairly well convinced that her grandmother had mistaken her meaning, but she refrained from making any more mention of the dress. That did not mean, however, that the beautiful rose ball gown was not foremost in her mind. That feeling of unease she had known upon leaving the house had since grown into a feeling of distinct discomfort. She heartily wished she had offered up a protest over the dress. At the very least, she thought, she should have insisted upon a gown of more demure design that would not have been so costly. Now it was too late—the purchase had been made—and she didn't care to think of the anger she would see in Owen's expression once he saw the bill from the *modiste*.

Mrs. Kendrick led the way through the door of another shop, where she insisted upon a new pair of slippers for Pen that would compliment the dress they had just purchased. From there, they entered yet another shop where Mrs. Kendrick had Pen's small hands measured for a new pair of gloves.

Pen had moved away toward the window of the shop and was worriedly tallying her rapidly mounting debt in her head when Augusta came to stand beside her, saying, "You are very lost in your thoughts, cousin. Tell me, are you thinking how very much you shall appear to advantage in your new finery?"

"I would rather not have any finery at all," she said sincerely. "I have a perfectly good dress that earned me some very nice compliments at a neighborhood cotillion I attended with Aunt Jane. Surely, that dress shall suffice. Surely all these new things are not necessary!"

"What a goose you are!" said Augusta, laughing slightly. "Of course they are necessary, if you are to meet the prince."

"But they are much too dear! I am certain the expense of all these new things is much more than I could ever afford!"

"But you are not to pay for them, silly girl. Owen shall settle the reckoning, just as he did when Grandmama purchased the gowns I wore for my London season." She studied Pen's face for a moment. "You still look worried. You shouldn't be, for Grandmama will take care of everything, mark my words!"

"But Owen shall think—"

"You must not tease yourself over what Owen may or may not think," said Augusta, with authority. "I am certain he can well afford to be generous for once in his life. You must leave the matter in Grandmama's hands."

Pen declined to follow her cousin's advice. The probable cost of the ball gown weighed heavily on her mind, and she dared not think what Owen's reaction would be once her grandmother confessed the cost of the thing. A vision of Owen, staring down at her grandmother with that same look of cold condemnation he had cast at Peter, only added to her guilt. By supper time she was admittedly worried over Owen's reaction and the clear possibility that her grandmother might not emerge the better from a confrontation with him.

She was determined to save her grandmother such a scene and decided there was nothing for it but that she, more than anyone, should suffer Owen's anger over an extravagant purchase.

She found Owen in the library, established in a comfortable chair with a book open in his lap. At his invitation, she sat down on a chair drawn close beside his and said in a rush, "I shall not beat about the bush, cousin. I have come to make a confession."

With a slight frown, he slowly closed the book and set it on a side table. "If you meant to capture my attention, Pen, you have succeeded. Tell me, what could you possibly have to confess?"

"We were shopping in Town today, Grandmama, Augusta, and I. We . . . we selected a ball gown for me at Grandmama's *modiste* . . ." Pen felt her voice fade under the cold weight of his gaze.

He waited for more, and when it was not forthcoming he prompted, "I am aware of your shopping expedition. Your grandmother discussed it with me this morning at breakfast."

"Yes, but I had thought . . . I never expected we would purchase . . . cousin, I fear the gown Grandmama ordered for me was horridly expensive!"

He was silent a moment, as if he were waiting for her to say more. "Is that it? Is that your confession?"

"There are gloves, as well, and we did purchase new dancing slippers, too. I . . . I fear I have cost you a great deal today, but I didn't know how to say no to Grandmama."

He was still frowning, which she found unnerving. Then his eyes narrowed as if he were unsure that he was seeing her correctly, and she felt as if his gaze might bore two holes right through the middle of her forehead. She lowered her gaze and fiddled with the fringe of her shawl as it draped across her arms.

He stood up suddenly and crossed to the window. He looked out for a long moment and said, "Do you know, I am not usually wrong about people. In fact, I fancy myself an excellent judge of character, but in this case—"

"I am sorry, Cousin Owen," she said in a small voice. "Are you very much disappointed in me?"

He turned back to her. "Not at all, but I am a good deal surprised. You are the first person of my acquaintance, other than Robert Carswell, who has ever shown me such consideration. After this morning, when we were riding and you spoke of moving in society and attending assemblies, I fully expected you to plague me by begging for one thing after another. I expected you to add your voice to the chorus of demands for jewels and pin money and carriages, and anything else that struck your fancy. I expected . . . well, I see now that it doesn't matter what I expected, for I was wrong."

"Are you saying you are not angry with me?"

"Not at all," he answered solemnly.

"Then will you help me tell Grandmama that the gown is too dear, too expensive to be purchased?"

"You may leave the matter with me. I shall take care of it with your grandmother."

There was something a little bit final about the way he spoke those words. She rose to her feet and moved toward the door. "Thank you. It is a lovely gown, and I think it would look well on me, but Aunt Jane was very clear to me that I was not to be a charge on you or Grandmama, and since I can ill afford the gown myself I cannot ask another to bear the cost of it."

"I understand." He said no more, but ushered her toward the door and kindly held it open for her. She ventured to peep at him for one fleeting moment, and thought she saw the merest of smiles on his lips.

Chapter Six

"How long have you worked at Rosemount, Tom?" asked Pen the next morning as she watched Tom Hawkins position the saddle on Little Angel's back.

"I've worked at Rosemount all my life, Miss. It was I that gave the master his first boost up on a horse's back, and it was I as taught him to take his first fence."

"Someone once said you can learn a lot about a man by the horse he rides."

"True enough," said Tom, nodding his head wisely. "You take Master Owen's horse—strong and with a mind of its own, but he knows what's expected of him and does it without complaining."

"Is that how you see Owen?" she asked, in some surprise.

"Aye. I've been here long enough to have seen him when he was a carefree young man, and I've seen him after old Mr. Kendrick died, when he looked like he had the weight of the world on his shoulders. He has had to step into his father's shoes, so to speak, and he's done so very ably, I should say."

She hadn't expected to hear such a tribute from a groom who had proved to be quite reticent on other matters. "Do you like working for my cousin? Is he a kind employer?"

"There's no one else I would rather work for, that's the truth. He's a fair man and generous. A groom can't ask for more in this world."

Tom threw her up on the saddle and followed her out of the stable yard at a discreet distance. Little Angel fidgeted and seemed anxious for a gallop, but Pen controlled her. She had lost her enthusiasm for a morning ride, and found herself wishing that her conversation with Tom had never taken place. His confidences only seemed to confuse her. How, she wondered, could Owen be such a good man if everyone else thought he was bad? How could his employees think him generous when his cousins believed him to be tightfisted in the extreme?

As she approached the meadow she saw a lone rider in the distance and immediately recognized Owen. He sent his horse galloping toward her. As she watched him approach, she had to admit he was a fine horseman, indeed.

"Good morning, cousin!" he said as he pulled alongside her. "I see you will insist on riding out on Little Angel."

Despite his choice of words there didn't seem to be any censure in Owen's tone, which gave Pen the courage to say, "She is a marvelous horse, Owen, and

I like riding her. It would seem your fears are for naught.''

He eyed her appraisingly for a moment. "I'll see Miss Hamilton back when she is ready, Tom." He was about to say more, but a nearby rustling in the grass—caused, no doubt by the movement of some small animal—caused Little Angel to shy. Owen's hand shot out, but not before Pen had brought the horse under control: "I told you that animal is not a proper mount for you. She's too dangerous and unpredictable."

"Nonsense. She is merely itching to gallop, as am I. Only see if you can keep up with us!" she challenged as she set Little Angel flying across the meadow. It wasn't long before she heard the sound of hooves thundering close behind her and Owen's horse drew abreast of hers. Before very long she had to admit she was terribly outdistanced.

Owen pulled up at last and she joined him, saying with breathless happiness, "What a perfect gallop that was! In fact, I think that everything about your life must be perfect indeed!"

He looked over at her, a laugh of surprise upon his lips and a confounded expression in his eyes. "Perfect? My life? Why do you say that?"

"Because you have so much. Tell me, what could be better than to gallop across your own land attached to your own magnificent estate, on a horse that must be the envy of four counties?"

He wheeled his horse around to walk alongside Pen's. "I never thought of it in quite those terms, but I see what you mean."

"You have so much. Your life at Rosemount must be a happy one."

"I don't think my life is better or worse than anyone else's. At present I daresay my family and I go on comfortably."

"I have heard Rosemount was a different place when your father was alive. Is that true?"

"Yes, things were very different," Owen said, quietly.

"I wish I had known your father, for everyone speaks well of him. Tell me, what kind of man was he?"

At first she didn't think he would reply, so long was he silent. At last he said, "My father was a good man who took pride in his family and took seriously his responsibilities. He loved your grandmother, you know, and generously brought her grandchildren to live here."

"Are you speaking of Peter and Augusta?"

"Yes. If your grandmother had applied to him, he would have had you and your aunt Jane to live here, too. He was generous, but not extravagant, for he ran Rosemount successfully. It is, I think, the premier estate in the area. That is part of the reason the prince is on good terms with Peter. To know the residents of Rosemount carries a certain caché."

"Augusta said that the entire east wing of Rosemount has been closed."

He looked upon her with one brow raised. "It has. That wing is in disrepair, and has the potential to be dangerous."

"Aren't the ballroom and the long gallery located there?"

"They are, but I must ask that you not venture off to see them until the needed repairs have been made."

There was something about the way he spoke that told Pen he was being evasive. She asked suddenly, "Cousin, are we poor?" It was an abrupt question, perhaps even a rude one, but it was out of her mouth before she could stop it.

Owen drew his horse to an abrupt halt and stared at her for a moment. "You're very blunt!"

"I beg your pardon, for I didn't intend to ask such a question. Both Grandmama and Augusta told me I must never discuss money, but I thought—that is, I merely wondered—you must admit the family does seem to argue about money quite a bit!"

"It wasn't always so. There was a time when the Kendricks were wealthy, indeed."

"Will you tell me what might have happened to change that?"

He said slowly, "Everything was changed by one man—a highwayman with a penchant for speaking in rhyme."

For a moment, she could only stare at Owen. She didn't want to hear such tales, and she certainly didn't want to believe them. "You are wrong," she said at last. "You only wish to blame another for your troubles and you have settled upon The Black Bard as your target."

"How staunchly you defend him! I wonder why

you are so quick to make excuses for a man who makes his way in the world by robbing innocent people."

"He only does so because he must! How else may he fight injustice in the world?"

"How may he do *what?*"demanded Owen, incredulously. "Is that what you think? That your precious highwayman is some kind of Robin Hood, who steals from the rich to give funds to the poor? Is that what you think?"

"He told me so himself!" defended Pen hotly. "He said he was taking my jewels for a noble purpose!"

"There are men in this world who think draining a tankard of ale is a noble purpose, but it doesn't follow that society thinks so, as well," he answered bitingly.

"You wouldn't say such things if ever you met the man."

"My dear cousin," he said with deadly calm, "if ever I have the chance to get my hands on The Black Bard you may be sure that I shall be the last person he ever meets."

From his words and the manner in which he spoke them, Pen was convinced that his was not an idle threat. Aghast, she demanded, "Do you mean to tell me you would kill him? Are you saying you would actually take the life of a man who never did you any harm?"

He didn't reply, but she saw that telltale muscle in his jaw tighten, signaling that he was controlling himself with an effort. At last he said, in an evenly mastered tone, "I can only hope that you are too innocent, too naive, to understand what you are saying, Pen. You are, I think, a naturally optimistic young woman, and I did think that a charming quality about you, initially. But I also see that your optimism can be dangerous, as well. I fear your way of looking at the world will one day land you in a great deal of trouble."

For a moment she didn't know whether to be gratified or offended, but when Owen followed up that speech by advising her that she was too willing to blindly trust in too many people, she retorted, "And you trust no one! And that, I think is the greater crime. In fact, I can think of no more horrid way to go through life, cousin!"

They returned to the stables in silence, still visibly angry with each other. They reached the stable yard to find Tom waiting for them and Mrs. Kendrick's little white dog, Candace, following close upon Tom's heels. As Tom helped Pen from her saddle Candace ran forward to greet them, yapping excitedly.

It was immediately evident to all that Little Angel resented the presence of the dog. She lifted both front hooves from the ground in warning, and when Candace offered a sharp bark of reprimand the horse took immediate and unforgiving exception. She reared again, just as Pen was alighting. One of Pen's feet was still in the stirrup, one foot was on the ground. In an instant, Pen felt herself falling as Little Angel suddenly bolted.

Pen hit the ground hard. Her foot twisted in the

stirrup, and before she knew what was happening she felt herself being dragged across the yard.

Still mounted, Owen positioned his own horse across Little Angel's path, preventing her from careening out beyond the confines of the stable yard. Tom rushed forward and grabbed Little Angel's bridle.

"Hold that blasted horse, Tom!" Owen commanded as he leapt down to the ground. He loosed Pen's foot from the stirrup and bent solicitously over her, saying, "Good God, Pen, are you all right? Are you seriously injured?"

She was definitely bruised and a good deal shaken, and it was a trembling hand that she placed in his as he made a move to help her to her feet. "I am not seriously hurt, I think. What happened? Everything occurred so quickly! In one moment I had a foot on the ground and in the next I was being dragged halfway across the yard!"

"It was that damned horse and her blasted tricks! I knew I should never have let you ride her! Your grandmother's dog spooked her a little, I think, and she panicked."

With Owen's assistance, Pen stood, but she let out a cry as a shard of pain traveled the length of her leg.

"You *are* injured," said Owen as he scooped her up in his arms. "Let us hope it is merely a sprain, and nothing more."

He set off toward the house, his arms about Pen as she rode high against his chest.

Her foot hurt like the very devil, but she said

bravely, "I can try to walk with your assistance, if I am too heavy to carry."

"Not at all," he said.

"Thank you for saving me. If it had not been for you, Little Angel might have dragged me for miles! Had you not intervened, I would have been seriously injured, indeed."

"In the future, perhaps you will be more compliant when I advise you, cousin. You never should have been on that horse in the first place." He paused a moment, then said, "Forgive me. That was unfair. I never should have said such a thing to you."

Her ankle was throbbing and her spirits were low. She said dismally, "I deserved it."

"Nonsense. Where is that optimistic spirit of yours I have come to appreciate?"

"You didn't appreciate it earlier today," she reminded him. "In fact, you said my optimism will lead me to trouble one day."

He looked down at her and she was a little taken aback by how close his face was to hers. He said, "I was wrong, Pen. I was speaking in anger, and I should never do so. Usually, I control my temper very well, but sometimes it will get the best of me. Am I forgiven?"

There was an expression in his eyes she had never seen before, an odd mixture of softness and intensity that she found rather hypnotic. It took every bit of willpower she possessed to look away, but she managed to do so and say in a credibly even voice, "Of course!"

"Excellent! Now, let us get you to your room and

have a doctor in to examine your foot. We can only hope it is a minor injury that will not prevent you from wearing those new dancing slippers you were telling me about."

Chapter Seven

The doctor proclaimed Pen's most serious injury to be nothing but a minor sprain and recommended a day of bed rest and a week of limited walking before she would find herself as good as new. Pen's abigail made a gratifying fuss over her injuries and assisted the doctor in bathing her scrapes and scratches and affixing poultices to the bruises on her back, arms, and shoulders.

Mrs. Kendrick, too, made a suitable fuss over Pen's predicament and scolded her dear little Candace for having been the cause of such a ghastly scene. Since she followed that stricture by feeding Candace morsels of food from her luncheon plate, however, the family was left to wonder how much of the scolding the dog actually took to heart.

Augusta visited her later in the day and found Pen

sitting up in bed, nestled against a collection of pillows and cushions.

"I have brought you some books to read. Shall I keep you company for a while, or would you rather sleep?"

"Please stay!" answered Pen immediately. "I am not at all used to such solitude and inactivity."

"Does your foot pain you very much?"

"Not always, and then I think I should like to be up and about and busy at life. No sooner do I make up my mind to get out of bed and move just the tiniest bit toward the edge of the mattress than my ankle is uncomfortable, indeed."

"Owen said he thought you were more injured than you let on. I heard him tell Peter that if you were seriously hurt he meant to shoot the horse that dragged you."

Pen gasped. "He couldn't have meant it!"

"I don't think so, but he was angered that he wasn't able to prevent what happened. He told Peter that if the two of you hadn't been arguing he might have been more alert to your horse's pranks."

"He couldn't have. No one can predict the actions of a skittish horse. It was my own fault for insisting on riding Little Angel, when Owen very plainly told me she was not to be trusted."

"Is that what you and Owen were arguing about?"

"No, we were disagreeing once again over The Black Bard."

"The highwayman who robbed you?"

"Yes. Merely because he stole my jewels doesn't make him a criminal."

Augusta cast her look that conveyed the possible notion that Pen might have lost her mind. "Cousin, I believe that stealing *is* criminal!"

"Yes, but the poor man only does so because he must. Yet Owen believes he is a blackguard, a man of low morals and no honor. Augusta, it simply isn't true!"

"You are very passionate on this subject! Tell me, how can you be so convinced of a highwayman's heart?"

Pen hesitated and fiddled for a moment with the fringe on the rug that covered her legs. "If I tell you, you must pledge it shall remain a secret between the two of us."

"Of course!"

"No, you must swear."

Augusta drew her fingers over her heart in the shape of a cross and said solemnly, "I swear."

Pen took a deep breath and decided there was no point in beating about the bush. She said simply, "He kissed me."

Augusta frowned. "Who did?"

"The Black Bard."

"Never!" breathed Augusta, deeply shocked.

"It's true. When he finished robbing my carriage, he bent down and kissed me." She allowed Augusta a few moments of silence in which to digest this startling news before she said, "Cousin, it was the most romantic and thrilling moment of my life. He was charming and dashing. He called me his little brown wren, and he said I had captured his heart."

"Goodness! It sounds very much as if the man is in love with you!"

"But is that possible? We saw each other for only minutes. Yet I must confess I have thought of little else ever since."

"Do you think you are in love with him, too?"

"I don't know. I don't even know how to tell if I am in love."

"I'll tell you how! You know you are in love when you can think of nothing else but the man you are in love with. You cannot concentrate, and the simplest tasks can fall into confusion. You lose your appetite, and find yourself pining for the merest glimpse of him. That, cousin, is how you know you are in love!"

"Is that how it is for you?" Pen asked gently.

At first Augusta did not reply. Then she said in a quiet voice, "I have been in love with Robert Carswell since I was a child. He is wonderful, isn't he?"

"He is indeed, and I think he is in love with you, too. So what is to prevent you from making a match of it?"

"Owen. I told you before that he controls everything—and he will try to control you, too!"

"Augusta, I cannot believe that."

"No? He sent me to London to find a wealthy husband instead of allowing me to marry the man I love."

"But why would he do such a thing?" asked Pen, clearly doubtful of Augusta's story.

"Owen wishes me to contract an alliance that will restore our family fortune. Robert Carswell is a gentleman of comfortable income, but he hasn't a vast fortune by any means."

"Augusta, I am certain you must be wrong about this!"

"Am I? When Grandmama took me to London for my season, Owen took me aside just before we boarded the carriage and told me he expected great things from me. He said the happiness of everyone depended upon the marriage I chose."

Pen had to admit that these words—if Owen had, in fact, uttered them—did lean a bit toward the mercenary. "It is hard to believe Owen could mean such a thing."

"Oh, he meant it!" August exclaimed bitterly. "He is not content to merely control our finances and order us about—he must rule my heart, as well!"

"Can Owen truly be as odious as you describe him?" asked Pen, clearly doubtful.

"Yes," said Augusta, after a moment of thought, "yes, I believe he is. You don't know how much our circumstances have changed since Owen's father died and Owen became the head of the family. We have been forced to live on the merest allowances, and the entire family has been forced to make enormous sacrifices."

"What kind of sacrifices?"

"Well, for instance, I have stopped buying trinkets and jewelry, and Grandmama no longer purchases jewels on a whim. But poor Peter suffers the worst, I fear, for he has had to give up many of his gentlemanly pursuits. Why, he visits his favorite gaming hells no more than three times a week now!"

Pen laughed. "That doesn't sound like sacrifice to me!" Nor, she thought, did the ogre Augusta described sound at all like the man whose company she had come to enjoy on her morning rides. At least, she amended, she enjoyed his company when they were not arguing.

When she thought, too, about Tom Hawkins and the things he had said about Owen, she was left to wonder how one man could be so differently judged.

In her own mind, she had thought him a man of honor. In all their dealings he had seemed fair, and not above apologizing in order to keep peace in their relationship. Augusta's confidences concerning Owen's character plagued her through the remainder of the day. Mrs. Kendrick visited her that evening, and Peter even obliged her by standing in the doorway and asking after her knee. Pen kindly corrected him, saying that it had been her foot which was injured, and he took that news with a look of solemn concern.

By morning Pen was weary of lying abed, and despite Betty's protests she instructed her maid to help her into her riding kit. Her legs and arms were bruised and her back and shoulders were stiff and scraped, but Pen was able to hobble about her room to prepare for her morning ride.

"I wish you would reconsider, Miss," said Betty in a tone of heavy disapproval. " 'Tis only foolish to walk on that foot afore it's healed."

"But the doctor told me to walk on it," Pen reminded her. "You were standing right there at the time he said it."

"To walk about your room is one thing. To trek out to the stables and climb back aboard that beastly animal is an entirely different matter!"

"Then you have one less thing to worry about,

Betty, for I will not be riding Little Angel today. I daresay I shall be lucky to ride out on docile old Phoebe. But ride I will, you may depend upon it!''

Betty helped Pen down the stairs and across the way to the stable, all the while maintaining a steady stream of criticisms and warnings of dire consequences if Miss Pen should insist upon making good her plan to ride out on this of all days.

Tom Hawkins was visibly surprised to see her, but he didn't offer up any protest when Pen politely asked him to saddle Phoebe.

"Is my cousin Owen already riding, Tom?"

"Yes, miss. I threw him up on Pharoah's back not more than half an hour ago," said Tom. Mindful of her injured foot, he led Phoebe over to a mounting step and assisted Pen up onto her saddle.

"Thank you, Tom. I shall catch up to my cousin," Pen said as she cantered out of the yard and directed her horse toward the meadow.

It would, she decided, be a very short ride, for even on the back of the meek Phoebe her injured foot was jostled into a dull ache.

After a short ride she saw Owen in the distance and she waved to him. He came to her quickly and said as he drew abreast of her, "Either you have made a remarkable recovery, or you have twice as much pluck as I thought you had. Are you certain you should be riding today?"

"Mine shall not be a long ride, I assure you," she said, "and Phoebe has promised not to make any more sudden moves than an occasional flick of her tail."

Owen smiled at her. It was the first time she had seen him do so, and she was struck by how handsome he was. Suddenly feeling flustered, she looked away for a moment. When she looked back she saw that his eyes were still upon her, and that strange light was once again dancing in their depths.

"Phoebe is a good horse that will do right by you," he said. "You were wise to take her out today. Unfortunately, I must return to the house. I have an appointment with one of my stewards. But I shall send Tom back to ride with you. You must only promise you shall not do too much and cause yourself even greater injury."

"I am following the doctor's orders with strictest obedience," she assured him.

"Are you? I had pegged you for a young lady who was always refreshingly *dis*obedient!"

She thought to protest, but stopped when she saw that he was smiling.

"Don't go far," he told her, "and I shall send Tom out to you."

With a quick touch to the brim of his hat, Owen sent his horse galloping back toward the stable and Pen began walking Phoebe in the opposite direction. After a while she turned and spent some moments admiring the view and the glorious grounds of Rosemount. She could readily understand why Owen rode every morning. If such a magnificent estate belonged to her, she would be sorely tempted to survey it every day, too.

In the distance she spied a lone rider, and she thought it might be Tom. She set her heels against

Phoebe's ribs and began to make her way across the meadow. But as she approached, she realized her mistake. She knew in an instant that it was not Tom she saw, although there was something vaguely familiar about the rider. He was dressed in dark clothing and was astride a horse of equally dark coloring, so it was difficult to tell where one being ended and the next began. The rider leaned forward in his saddle, and as Pen watched he slumped slightly, then tumbled down to the ground.

She spurred her horse onward and reached him in an instant. Gathering her skirts about her, Pen slid off her horse and hobbled over to where the rider was lying facedown in the clover.

For a moment she didn't know what to do. She took a quick, desperate look about, hoping that someone would come and help. In the distance she saw Tom Hawkins riding toward her at brisk trot, but she dared not wait for him. She turned her attentions to the barely conscious man.

"Sir? Sir! Are you injured?" she asked of the figure on the ground in a gentle voice.

She received no answer to her question and bent down, the better to examine him. "Sir, if you are hurt I shall help you, but you must tell me what the matter is."

Receiving yet again no answer, Pen reached down and carefully pulled at the sleeve of the black driving coat. As the rider slowly turned over onto his back, Pen let out a gasp. The man's face was pale and his brow was furrowed, and his mouth was set in a grim line from pain, yet she recognized him. So often had he haunted her dreams, so often had his image filled her waking memories. She would have recognized The Black Bard anywhere.

The shoulder and sleeve of his coat were bloody, and Pen judged the heavy garment covered a rather serious wound. "Oh, sir, you are gravely injured! Only tell me how you have been hurt!"

He opened his eyes slightly then and focused a dazed glance upon her face. After a moment, he favored her with that same slight, half-smile that had so enchanted her a few evenings before. "Ah, it is my little brown wren who has found me."

So, he remembered her! Pen couldn't have felt more gratified, but she curbed her emotion and said in a gentle tone, "You mustn't speak now. You must conserve your strength."

"Conserve my strength? Why? So I may swing more heartily from Tyburn Tree after you have turned me over to the magistrate?"

"Never say such a thing!" exclaimed Pen. "I would never do such a thing! You must trust me, sir. I swear no harm shall come to you. I shall nurse you back to health myself. I shall summon a physician to care for you!"

His hand clasped hers, and even in his weakened state his grip was urgent and powerful. "No physician! I cannot risk it. Swear to me you will not tell anyone of this. Swear!"

Since Tom Hawkins chose that moment to draw his horse up close upon them and leap to the ground, Pen thought it was rather too late to make such a promise. "But how am I to help you without telling someone? Here is Tom Hawkins, and I know he will help us. I know he may be trusted with our secret."

Tom knelt beside her and ran a cursory glance over the length of the injured man's body. "What have we here now, Miss Hamilton?"

"I've just come upon this man, Tom, and he's injured. Do you think you can help him?"

"I can try, but I cannot do very much for him in a meadow, miss. First thing, we must get the gentleman to the house, I think."

Pen felt the Bard's fingers close tighter about hers until she almost cried out. She tried to reassure him, saying, "Sir, you must not worry. Tom can be trusted."

"Make him swear," ordered the Bard through pale lips. "Make him swear!"

"Tom, you must promise you shall tell no one of this. You must swear you shall never speak of it to *anyone.*"

Tom sat back on his heels and rubbed his grizzled chin thoughtfully. "Here, now, Miss Hamilton, I cannot give an assurance like that. Master Owen must be told if there's an injured man brought into his house."

"No, Tom, you mustn't. I cannot explain it to you now, but you must believe there is a very good reason for me to demand your word that you will not speak of this. Please? It is very important."

"No, miss. I don't see how we can keep this a secret. You're asking me to help hide a wounded man in plain sight, so to speak. Someone of the family or household is bound to stumble upon him, no matter what bedchamber we stow him in."

"What about the east wing? No one shall find him if we put him there. Owen sealed that part of the house off long ago, and the family is forbidden to go there. Owen told me so himself."

Tom Hawkins bore the expression of a man who couldn't quite decide whether to steadfastly follow his duty to his employer or succumb to the pleading look in a pair of limpid brown eyes. If he needed encouragement Pen was willing to give it to him, and she said rather sorrowfully, "Of course, if we leave him in this meadow for very much longer, we shall not have to worry about Owen, or anything but a proper burial for the poor man. Then you and I shall be left to live with our consciences and rue the day we failed to help a poor traveler who was injured and weak."

"Now, Miss Hamilton, I didn't say I wouldn't help—"

"Then that means you will," she countered, seizing upon the logic of his words. She turned her attentions back to the injured man, saying, "Sir, you are as good as healed. Tom Hawkins promises he shall never breathe a word of your situation to anyone, don't you, Tom?"

"Well, miss, I can't very well leave the man to die, now, can I?"

"There! Tom is sworn to secrecy. He shall help us. You must be very brave, sir, for we shall have to move you and I fear the jostling will be painful for you."

The injured man's eyes fluttered closed as he murmured, "My little brown wren, I knew you captured my heart for a reason." He loosened his grip upon her hand and was silent after that—a circumstance Pen thought to be for the best, for she suspected The Black Bard would have been in considerable pain had he been awake during the next few minutes.

Tom took extra care with him, but there was no easy way to hoist the injured man over the back of Tom's horse. Even in his unconscious state, the man moaned once or twice as Tom and Pen moved him. When his limp body was at last draped over the back of the horse, Pen noticed that the bloodstain on his coat had deepened and spread even farther down his sleeve.

She could never have managed the injured man without Tom Hawkins. As The Black Bard's prone figure balanced precariously over the back of his horse, Tom slowly led the animal toward the manor house. Being familiar with the servants' routines, he knew which door was most likely to be unmanned, and he knew, too, the safest hall passages to take to avoid detection. Pen hurried about him, opening and closing doors for him as he carried the wounded man over his shoulder.

Pen hobbled about on her injured foot, trying to be as quiet as possible and fearing detection at every turn. Too late did she realize that to reach the bed-chambers in the east wing they would have to pass by the door to Owen's apartments. She tiptoed past his door, and Tom followed until they were at last safely past it and on their way to one of the farthest suites in the old east wing.

Tom deposited the man on top of a bed draped in Holland covers. Pen placed a cushion beneath his head and studied the man's pale face. A dusky curl had fallen over his brow, and she tenderly brushed it back. She noted the straight line of his aquiline nose, the masculine cut of his jaw, but it was his mouth that captured her attention. She had only to gaze upon those firm, handsomely curved lips to recall all over again the feeling of his kiss upon her mouth. She had almost convinced herself that she would never again see her handsome, charming highwayman, but he was there before her, injured and weak, and he needed her.

Tom interrupted her reverie, saying, "I think you would be best to go about your business now, Miss Hamilton."

"I couldn't, Tom. He needs me."

"He needs to be put to bed, miss, and that is not something I can do with you in the room, if you understand my meaning."

Pen meant to argue with him, but when Tom crossed the room and held the door open for her and favored her with a pointed look, she abandoned that plan. "You will tell me as soon as you have him settled, won't you?" she asked as she slowly inched across the threshold. "And you will be gentle with him, and take extra care when you examine his wound, and—"

"Miss Hamilton, the man could have no better care from his own mother, that's how careful I shall be. You may rely on me, miss."

With that he closed the door, leaving Pen alone in the old, deserted passageway.

Chapter Eight

"Penelope, dear, you are driving me to distraction!" said Mrs. Kendrick in a tone of deep exasperation. "You have done nothing but fidget since you first sat down at this breakfast table. What's more, you have been picking at your food for ten minutes and still you have not eaten one bite!"

Pen started guiltily. "I'm sorry, Grandmama," she said as she forced herself to put a forkful of food to her mouth.

"You do seem a bit agitated," said Augusta as she cast a probing look at Pen. "Is anything the matter?"

Pen forced a bright smile to her lips. "Nothing at all, I assure you. I think my foot is paining me a little, and my shoulders are still a bit sore. I was thinking of going back to my room for a little while."

"It was that tumble from the horse that did it," pronounced Mrs. Kendrick. "You were, I think, more seriously injured than we knew. I had thought to ask you to accompany me into Brighton, but I see now that would be a mistake.''

If forced to tell the truth, Pen would have admitted that her ankle was much improved, but since she was much more anxious to spend the day with the dashing man of her dreams than with her grandmother, she grasped the excuse. ''Thank you, Grandmama. I think I would be better served to rest for a while in my room.''

Mrs. Kendrick quickly agreed that Pen's health would be none the better for a drive into Town and enlisted Augusta's promise to accompany her, instead.

No sooner was Pen left alone in the dining room than she picked up her breakfast plate, spread a linen napkin over it, and limped her way toward the east wing. She rapped lightly upon the door of the once deserted bed chamber to signal her presence, then entered the room. Tom Hawkins was seated in a chair drawn near to the bed, and stood as soon as she entered.

''How is he faring, Tom? Is he better?'' she asked as she set the plate of food upon a table and turned her attention upon the man in the bed.

''It's too soon to say, miss. He's lost blood, and his color doesn't look good at all.''

''Has he asked for me?''

''No, miss. The lad hasn't woke once since we brought him in.''

Alarmed, Pen's eyes flew to Tom's face. ''You don't

think he will die, do you? He musn't! He cannot die, Tom!''

"Now, miss, there's no good barking at a dog that won't bite, if you see my meaning. He's a young lad and strong enough, I should think. You must give him time to heal.''

"Are his wounds very serious?'' Pen asked, although she was fearful of the answer.

"He took a bullet in his shoulder, but it looks to me that it went straight through and out his back. It's a nice, clean wound, I think, and one that should heal with proper rest.''

Pen sat down in the chair by the bed and examined the face of the unconscious man, willing him to open his eyes or raise a brow or even sigh deeply in his sleep. He did none of those, and she felt a twinge of worry stab at her heart. His handsome face was peaceful and his brow was smooth and clear, free of the furrowed grimace that had marred his features earlier that morning.

"When do you think he will awaken?'' she asked, rather wistfully.

"These things take time, Miss Pen. I suspect he'll open his eyes when nature tells him to. I'll stay with him as long as I can, but he'll have to be left alone for a spell while I tend to stable duties.''

"But he cannot be left unattended. What if he awakens? What if he is frightened or disoriented? If you must go about your duties, I shall stay with him— all day, if need be.''

"That will never do,'' said Tom with a firm shake of his head. "You'll be missed long before anyone misses me. No, I suspect if you wish this business to remain a secret you shall have to make up your mind right now that you may only visit the young man from time to time.''

''But, Tom—''

''Only think what will happen, miss. What if the family were to discover you gone and go looking for you? They'd sooner or later find you or the young man. Your secret would be nothing but a memory then, now wouldn't it?''

''I see your point,'' she said grudgingly. ''Only promise me you shall not leave him for very long at a time. I . . . I shall worry over him.''

''I promise, miss.'' Tom went to the door and opened it expectantly.

''If he should awaken and if he should ask for me, you will fetch me right away, won't you?'' asked Pen as she began a slow pilgrimage toward Tom and the open door.

''Yes, miss.''

''And if he should ask for anything—anything at all!—you will be sure to let me know?''

''I give you my word, miss.''

''Thank you, Tom.''

He held the door as she passed through it. When she turned and hesitated, he asked, ''I don't suppose, miss, you would wish to tell me *why* we must keep this business a secret?''

''I cannot tell you. But please believe that I wouldn't ask you to do so if it were not absolutely necessary.''

Tom considered this for a moment. ''Yes, miss,'' he said at last, ''but if you or the young man are in some sort of trouble, miss, you could do no better than to tell Master Owen. He's a good man who will help you, I think.''

"Thank you, Tom, but no one must know of this. No one! You gave me your promise, now."

"I did indeed, miss, and I won't go back on it."

She smiled and drew a breath of relief. "I knew I could trust you! I'll return as soon as I am able."

Pen hobbled down the hall toward the door that led off to the main part of the house. She was through the door and quietly making her way past Owen's rooms when the door to his suite flew open and Owen himself stepped out into the hall.

She came perilously close to colliding with him, and she let out a startled cry. His hands captured her shoulders and held her a moment, steadying her.

"Pen! Are you all right? You look as though you've seen a ghost," he said as he examined her face with concern.

For a moment she couldn't reply, so startled was she. Whether her present state of unnerve stemmed from the fact that Owen had discovered her exiting a forbidden wing of the house or from the feeling of his strong hands at her shoulders, she couldn't be sure. She was certainly breathless, and said, "You . . . you merely startled me, nothing more!"

"Still getting used to the house and where all the rooms are, are you? I think you are a little lost, young lady," he said. He gave her slim shoulders a reassuring squeeze before he released them. "I was just about to send the household out searching for you. Come, we're to assemble in the drawing room."

She found her voice at last. "But why?"

"Peter has great news for us."

"He . . . he does?"

"That's what he claims. Your grandmother and Augusta have not yet left for Town, and they are anxiously waiting for you so we may all hear Peter's announcement together."

His fingers lightly brushed her elbow to guide her toward the stair and Pen felt a little jolt, something on the order of an electric shock, course through her body. She took a deep breath and tried to calm her senses as she and Owen joined the rest of the family in the drawing room.

Mrs. Kendrick was seated in a chair by the fire, fidgeting with her gloves. Augusta, dressed most fetchingly in a matching bonnet and pelisse, sat side by side with Robert Carswell on a nearby settee. Peter had struck a commanding pose at the mantel. They looked round as the door opened; Robert rose to his feet.

"There you are at last, Penelope!" exclaimed Mrs. Kendrick. "Dear girl, we have been waiting on you for an age."

"I am sorry, Grandmama, but I had no idea you wished to see me."

"Well, you are here now, and dear Peter has something to say to us all, something quite important, I am sure!"

Pen dipped a quick curtsy toward Robert Carswell, prompting her grandmother to say, "You needn't stand on ceremony with Carswell, child. We quite consider him a member of the family. Why, we think of him almost as a brother to Peter and Augusta!"

"Tell us your news," said Owen as he ushered Pen to a chair.

Peter removed from his vest pocket a piece of fine linen paper, which he held aloft. "This was delivered to me this morning," he said in a tone of heavy significance. "It is from the prince, and he means to be in Brighton by the end of the week. He's opening The Pavilion." He paused dramatically, then said, "There is to be a ball, and we all are invited!"

There was a short silence in the room. Then all at once, everyone reacted to the news. Augusta sprang to her feet, an expression of happy disbelief on her face. Mrs. Kendrick gave an audible gasp, and Robert grinned broadly. Watching them, Pen found herself smiling, too. She chanced to look at Owen, who was standing a little way apart near the window. Unlike the rest of the family, he showed no reaction to the news except that his brows were knit together and his eyes were narrowed, as if he were in deep concentration. After a moment, his expression cleared, yet he remained the one member of the family who was not gladdened by Peter's announcement.

Mrs. Kendrick dropped her gloves in her lap and placed a fluttering hand to her heart. "My dear boy, are you quite certain we have received an invitation? Please, I must see it for myself!"

He smiled indulgently and obliged her by handing the paper over to her.

She scanned the sheet quickly. "It is true. It is from

the prince! My dears, I do believe this is the happiest day we have seen in some time!"

"I dare not believe we shall actually attend a royal ball!" breathed Augusta.

"It's true enough," said Peter, beaming benevolently upon them. "We are all going to The Marine Pavilion as guests of the prince."

Augusta had a sudden thought. "Peter, do you think we shall actually meet the prince? I shall be very nervous, indeed!"

"I am certain the prince shall speak to each of his guests," he said with a laugh, "but I shall ensure he takes notice of my only sister, as well as the rest of my family."

"Peter, you are the most wonderful brother in the whole world!" exclaimed Augusta as she launched herself into his arms.

"Will there be dancing, do you think?" asked Pen. "I do so love to dance."

"Then you must apply to Owen," said Robert Carswell, "for Owen is the finest dancer in the county."

Pen twisted slightly in her chair, the better to look over to where Owen was standing. "Are you?" she asked, in a clearly doubtful tone.

Those two words were out of her mouth before she could stop them, and she flushed slightly to think she had spoken so rudely. Owen didn't appear to be the least offended. Instead, his dark brows rose and his lips formed a slight smile. "Robert is always scrupulously honest. You should never doubt him."

"I didn't but . . . forgive me, but I cannot even imagine you on a dance floor, and now to be told you are an accomplished dancer—'' She stopped, laboring under the strong belief that the more she spoke the more deeply she slipped into the quagmire of discourtesy. She tried again. ''I am certain you are a most excellent partner.''

''That was very polite of you, but I can tell from your expression you are certain of no such thing,'' said Owen. He clasped her hand and drew her to her feet. ''I see you still doubt me. Robert, you had better clear that table away or Pen will worry that we shall topple it.''

No sooner was Pen standing before him than he slipped an arm about her waist. ''I hope your ankle is better, for you are about to go dancing, young lady,'' he said, and he began to move her rhythmically about the room.

Augusta happily clapped her hands together and quickly sat down at the pianoforte. ''Oh, you are dancing a waltz. Wait for me, for I know the music,'' she said as she began to play an accompaniment.

Owen gracefully navigated Pen about the room. After a few moments he said, in a rather low voice that only she could hear, ''Now do you believe Robert? Have I convinced you that I am an acceptable partner?''

As she looked up into his face she thought she detected a light of amusement in his eyes. ''I had no idea you could dance so well!''

''Surprised? You shouldn't be, for there are a great many things you don't know about me, Cousin Pen.''

''Indeed there are, and it makes me curious about you.''

His brows flew up. "You are curious? About *me?*"

"Yes, for I wonder sometimes what you are thinking. When Peter first announced the prince's invitation, for example. I was certain that you were frowning at first and looking rather grim. But then suddenly, when everyone started chattering, the frown was gone from your face and you were lighthearted, just like the rest of the family."

He stopped dancing then and looked down at her face for a moment before he removed his hand from about her waist. He drew her fingers, still clasped in his, to his lips in a brief salute and said, in a low voice, "Perceptive little Pen. How much *do* you see, I wonder?"

She hadn't the faintest idea what he meant by such a question, but she had no opportunity to ask. He moved away from her as Mrs. Kendrick said, "That was very prettily done, my dears. Owen, you must promise to lead Penelope out for at least one dance."

"Or, perhaps two," he said quietly from his place near the window.

Pen felt the telltale heat of a blush covering her cheeks and tried to dispel it by saying lightly, "That might not be wise, for while Cousin Owen is an excellent dancer, I am not. It was I who was forced to mind the steps. And I trod on his toes at least twice, I am certain!"

"Pen, you goose, you and Owen danced very well together," said Augusta with enthusiasm. "Grandmama, if we are to attend the prince's ball, I shall need new slippers."

"And I shall have a new headdress, I think," said

Mrs. Kendrick as she moved toward the door. "Come along, Augusta. There is no time to waste." She paused just before she left the room and looked back to say, in a wondrous tone, "My dears, this is happy news! You have no notion how much I have wished for this day!" Augusta and Peter went out with her.

Pen took her leave of Robert and Owen on the pretext of going to her room, but no sooner did she find herself alone in the hall than she immediately headed for the east wing.

The room in which she had hidden away the highwayman was in shadows and dimly lit, but she thought she detected a slight sound as she tiptoed toward the bed. "Sir? Sir, are you awake?" she asked softly.

At first she received no response. Then a weakened voice from the bed asked, "Who is there?"

She went quickly to his side. "It is I, Penelope Hamilton, sir. Are . . . are you feeling better?"

He smiled feebly and closed his eyes. "I had thought before you were nothing but a vision—I dared not trust you were real, my little brown wren."

She felt her cheeks go pink with pleasure. "I assure you, I am very real, sir. Tell me, are you comfortable? Is there anything I may give you that will ease your pain or speed your recovery?"

He closed his eyes and gave her question grave consideration. "Your name. What did you say your name was?"

"I am Pen Hamilton, sir. And what name may I call you?"

"James. Merely James, nothing more."

She turned that simple name over in her mind and

decided that it suited him very well. She would have liked to have asked him many more questions, but he looked so helpless, so weak and pale, that she hesitated. Still, there was one question she felt she had to ask of the man who had so haunted her dreams ever since the moment their paths had crossed. She asked, "Have you any family, sir? Is there anyone who will worry over your whereabouts? A family member? Or a . . . a *wife*, perhaps?"

He shook his head slightly and immediately winced. "No, there is no one. I make my way alone in the world, you see."

Pen felt a twinge of emotion clutch her heart. "You have someone now. I shall stay with you and you may remain here in this room as long as you need to—and longer, if you wish. You may rely on me and you may trust me, I swear."

He opened his eyes again and raised one hand to lightly brush his fingertips along her cheek. "You are, I think, an angel."

An angel? thought Pen. Hardly. But she did entertain the slight notion that the dusty old bedchamber had turned into a little piece of heaven.

If anything, the highwayman was even more handsome than he had been that evening on the road. And although his face was pale and his lips were pressed into a grim line, signaling his discomfort, she remembered very well the feeling of his lips on hers.

She remained with him as long as she could, but she was mindful of Tom's warnings that someone in the family might discover her missing. After a while, when he appeared to be sleeping soundly, she went back to her room.

Her grandmother and cousin returned from their shopping expedition, and Augusta came knocking at Pen's bedroom door. She proudly spread her purchases before Pen upon the bed, much as a peddler would spread his wares for inspection. Pen tried to show interest in Augusta's tales of the wonders of Brighton shops, but her attention was still on the highwayman and the state of his health.

It was late afternoon before Pen could return to the bedchamber in the east wing. The sun was setting low in the sky, sending shadows across the room, playing tricks of light upon the bedclothes. She looked at the figure in the bed and refused to believe her eyes. She took a step closer and looked again. Her highwayman was sitting up in bed, bolstered by a framework of pillows.

"You are awake!" she exclaimed, her eyes like stars. "And you are well, I think."

"Not well, but certainly I am better, thanks to you. Come, sit beside me and keep me company."

She could think of nothing she would rather do, and obediently claimed the chair beside the bed. "You must be very careful not to tire yourself, so that your wound heals properly. You have been shot, you know."

"How long have I been here?" he asked.

"Three days."

"Egad, that long? I must leave at once!" He made a move to throw the bedcovers aside and immediately his face creased into a line of pain and he sucked in his breath.

"You must not move," Pen adjured him. "You are very weak and seriously injured."

"But I must leave. If someone were to find me here—" He stopped short, and as if for the first time he took stock of his surroundings. "Where, exactly, am I?"

"Rosemount. This is the home of my grandmother and cousins."

He examined her face with a frown. "I'm familiar with the place, I think. Isn't the master of Rosemount a man by the name of Kendrick?"

"Yes, that is my cousin, Owen. Do you know him?"

"You might say I do. He has been a thorn in my side for a number of years. A more starched lip, priggishly moral man I have yet to meet!"

Pen shifted uncomfortably. "He is, I believe, somewhat conservative in his views—"

"Don't defend him," said the highwayman. "I have a notion you are always good and kind to anyone who needs it."

"I try to make people happy when I am able."

"You have made me happy, just by making yours the first face I saw when I awoke this morning."

Pen felt that telltale heat flush across the surface of her cheeks, but she tried to hide her fluttering nerves by saying, "You may stay here as long as you like. I swear you shall not be discovered."

He took another look around the room. "Is the house abandoned, then?"

"Only this wing. It has been closed for some time,

and you should be safe here. No one knows you are here except Tom and me."

"Who is Tom?"

"The head groom. He helped me bring you here, and you may trust him to keep your presence a secret. I shall ask him to bring you some dinner later tonight. And perhaps, if you like, I could come and read to you." She felt a wave of embarrassment as soon as the words escaped her lips. She should never have offered to do such a thing. She should never have volunteered to stay alone with an unattached, ridiculously handsome and perhaps even dangerous man. She felt in her heart, though, that she had nothing to fear from him. She was drawn to him, as a moth to a flame, and felt herself fighting back that little voice of caution in her head.

"I should like that, my little brown wren, more than you know."

She felt a wave of happiness wash over her, and it was all she could do to make herself leave his side with the promise that she would return as soon as she was able.

She moved quietly along the passageway and through the door that led to the main part of the house. She had tiptoed past the door to Owen's suite and was hurrying toward the stair before she realized that someone was there before her, someone climbing the stair and just reaching the passageway. She saw in an instant that it was Owen, and in the next moment he was before her, blocking her way and bringing her hurried steps to a halt.

Chapter Nine

A startled exclamation escaped her lips and she gripped the banister in an effort to calm her racing heart.

Upon seeing her coming down the passageway, Owen had stopped, but now he came striding toward her with slow, unhurried steps. He was frowning and studying her pale face in the dimming light of the late afternoon.

"Pen? What are you doing there?" he asked. There was no mistaking the suspicion in his voice.

She was so startled that for a moment she couldn't trust herself to speak.

"You were in the east wing, weren't you?" he asked, after a moment in which she had tried to calm her racing heart. "I told you, I think, that the east wing is closed."

"Yes, yes, you did, but—"

"You will do me the favor, I hope, of obeying my instructions in this matter, as the rest of the family does. No one is to go into the east wing of the house."

"Yes, Owen," she said, thinking that meekness might prove to be her best defense.

He looked at her a long moment. "I suppose there was no harm done, and I cannot blame you for being curious about the place. But I hope you will do as I ask, nevertheless."

"I am sorry, Owen. It won't happen again."

He seemed satisfied with that and stood aside then, allowing her to pass. "You'll find your grandmother in the drawing room. I think she was asking for you."

Anxious to remove herself from under Owen's alert eye, Pen moved quickly down the stairs to the drawing room. Mrs. Kendrick was there as Owen had said, seated at a small writing table and engaged in the business of listing all the people of her acquaintance to whom she should relay the happy news of the prince's invitation. She looked up as Pen came in. "There you are! You must write straightaway to your aunt Jane and tell her about the prince's ball. I want her to know exactly in what sort of circles you travel since you came to us!"

Pen gave a light laugh. "I think Aunt Jane shall be very pleased to hear the news."

"And after we have finished telling all our friends and loved ones our news, I shall make a list of everyone who has ever been mean to us. I intend that they, too, shall know of our good fortune, and I hope they will be beyond envious!"

"Oh, Grandmama, who could ever have been mean

to you?" asked Pen as she planted a light kiss upon the top of her grandmother's head.

"You would be surprised at how many people I once counted as friends have cut me since dear Mr. Kendrick died."

"But why would they do that?"

"Jealousy, I suppose. There was a time, you know, when the Kendricks were the leading family in the county. Our situation has changed remarkably since then, and there are those who see it as a significant step down." She paused then, and set her pen back in its casing. She said solemnly, "I think they may be right. I think, perhaps, the Kendricks are not the family we once were."

Pen sat down in a chair close beside the writing desk and regarded her grandmother with concern. "Why do you say that, Grandmama?"

"There are rumors about Town, you know, that we have become somewhat impoverished. And who can blame people for thinking so when we never entertain or send invitations to those who have invited us? I was thinking just now that perhaps this ball at The Pavilion may not be such a good thing for us, after all."

"Grandmama, how can you speak so? Why, we have all been in elation over the prospect of seeing The Pavilion and perhaps even meeting the prince!"

"Yes, but don't you see, my dear? If all of our acquaintances believe us to be poor, how shall I ever bear to face my old friends? I will not be an object of pity for them, nor will I suffer their gossip, I assure you!"

"Then do not. Simply don that new headdress you purchased and wear your best gown and ignore them."

"Yes, I suppose you are correct, my dear. But you know, I blame Owen for this whole mess. In my heart I have tried to be a good stepmama to him, and I cannot understand why he must insist upon returning my affection with petty punishments. He knows it is my dearest wish to hold a ball at Rosemount, much as we used to when Mr. Kendrick was alive, but he forbids me to host the merest card party."

"I am certain there must be a very good reason for that," said Pen, although she could not for the life of her think exactly what that reason might be. "Perhaps if you applied to him again?"

"He shall only forbid it again," said Mrs. Kendrick dismally.

"There must be a way for you to hold a party at Rosemount," said Pen. Other than speaking directly to Owen on the matter, though, she could think of no scheme that would bring about such a possibility. She suspected that any attempt she might make to discuss the subject with Owen might be construed as meddling. Later that evening when she went into the library to select a book to take up to James, she found Owen already there and quite alone. It was, perhaps, a kind of sign, she thought, that she should make an attempt to persuade him to give his permission for a ball.

She closed the door softly and waited for him to perceive her presence.

He was standing by the desk, staring at a portrait

of a very distinguished looking man. Seeing him so, she recognized in both Owen and the figure in the portrait the same nose, the same blue eyes, the same straight, broad-shouldered posture. She knew in an instant that the portrait was of Owen's father, but she could not perceive why he would merely stand, staring at it so.

So deep in his thoughts did he appear to be that she hated to interrupt him and stood quietly, waiting for him to realize her presence. When at last he did turn and look at her, he had about him, she thought, the look of one who was in the midst of making a momentous decision.

"Pen? I had no notion you were here. How long have you been standing there?"

"Not long, but I didn't wish to interrupt you. I can come back later if I am disturbing you."

"Not at all. Would you like to select a book?"

"Yes, but I would also like to speak with you about a matter of some importance. I had hesitated to talk to you before, but since we are both here it does seem providential. Perhaps you will listen to my request with charity."

"If you meant to gain my attention, you have succeeded!" he said, ushering her toward a chair. "Tell me, what is your request, Pen?"

"I wish to ask why you will not allow Grandmama to have a party or a ball at Rosemount."

His dark brows rose. "I see. Did your grandmother ask you to speak to me?"

"No, she didn't. Grandmama doesn't even know I am here with you."

"So you have come on your own to ask me to change my mind on a subject I have often spoken of with your grandmother? She is a tenacious woman."

"Perhaps, but she is also a woman who holds affection for you, and when you deny her without explanation the things she loves she is tempted to believe you do not care for her."

He looked at her sharply. "That is not true. Your grandmother has been very kind to me, and she made my father's life a happy one. For that I owe her a tremendous debt."

"Then will you not make her happy and allow her to host a ball at Rosemount?"

"Pen, you don't know what you are asking. I'm afraid it's not that simple."

"If you explain to me your reasons, I am certain I shall understand. Only please don't let Grandmama and the rest of the family believe you forbid them entertainments merely because you wish to be cruel."

"I would rather they thought me cruel than sense-less." He turned back toward the portrait again and looked at it for a few moments. When he turned back toward Pen and took a chair near hers, he had about him the look of one who had seen his fate and was resigned to it.

He leaned forward in his chair and rested his arms on his legs. He didn't look at her, but focused his gaze on his hands clasped together before him. He said, in a quiet voice, "There is no money, Pen."

"I don't understand. You live in luxury in a home of vast wealth."

"And we are about to lose that home. All our money

is gone, and has been for some time. After Augusta's season last year, I sold the London town house and the house at Tunbridge Wells, along with the hunting lodge. We have been living off the proceeds, but now that money is gone, too. There is no more. I had hoped that with economy and some added efficiencies we might be able to last a few more months, but now . . ."

His voice trailed away, prompting Pen to ask, "But why? What has changed?"

"The invitation. The expense of our attending the ball at The Pavilion will see the last of our funds. But even at that, I cannot deny your grandmother and cousins the treat. I saw the looks on their faces when Peter told them the news, and even though I know it will bankrupt us I cannot bring myself to forbid them to go."

He stood then, and took a rather distracted turn about the room.

Pen watched him in silence for a moment, then asked, gently, "Is that the reason there is no money to make the repairs in the east wing?"

"Oh, that," he said, rather ruefully. "There is nothing wrong with the east wing that needs repairing. I merely told the family it was in need of refurbishing so they would not question me when I closed it up. It was one of my economies, you see. But in the end, even that didn't help."

"Owen, how could such a thing happen?"

"I could tell you how, but you won't want to hear it!"

"Of course I shall listen, and willingly," she replied. "Tell me, won't you?"

"Have you never heard, then, the story of how my father died? It's a simple tale. My father was an innocent man traveling down a country road. Not far from his destination, he was set upon by a high-wayman."

Of a sudden, Pen felt her throat constrict. "Oh, no!" she murmured, not sure that she wanted to hear the rest of his tale.

"It's true, I'm afraid. He was coming back from London, riding—perhaps, foolishly!—alone. He was less than three miles up the Brighton Road from here when he was accosted. He was robbed of everything—his jewels, his cash, and the bearer bonds he was carrying. Those bonds represented the majority of our wealth. Without them, we haven't the money to continue on."

Despite the thumping of her heart in her breast, Pen managed to ask, "The highwayman—did he—he didn't shoot your father, did he?"

"No, but the shock of the robbery proved to be too much for my father's heart. Robert Carswell and I found him lying on the side of the Brighton Road, where the highwayman had left him. He was still alive, but barely. We brought him back to Rosemount, and he died the next day. But before he passed away he told me how the highwayman had taunted him by speaking to him in rhyme."

Horrified, Pen brought her fingers up to cover her mouth. "I cannot believe it!" she murmured, but in her heart she knew Owen was telling her the truth. "Why have you never spoken of this to anyone?"

"Robert knows, but I made the decision to keep the news of our financial predicament from the family. I thought if I were frugal and managed carefully we would be able to carry on, although in much more straightened circumstances. I was wrong."

"You cannot blame yourself for this, Owen," she said, going to him and laying a comforting hand upon his arm. "None of this is your doing or your fault."

"I know. Still, your grandmother depended upon me and I cannot help feeling I have let her down, somehow."

"Is there nothing that can be done?"

"Without those bearer bonds, we have nothing to look forward to but bankruptcy, I'm afraid."

They stood side by side in silence for a moment, with Pen acutely aware of her hand, still on his arm. When he placed his own hand over hers and held it there, she recognized a strong feeling of tenderness toward him.

"Thank you for confiding in me. I shall not repeat what you have told me, but I think you are in error to keep such a secret. The family must be told."

"After the prince's ball I shall speak to Peter. Together we will find a way to tell your grandmother. She'll be deeply hurt, I know."

"But she will also be relieved, I think, to hear the reason behind your behavior. She is beginning to believe you will not allow her to hold a party at Rosemount because you have taken her in dislike!"

That confidence brought a slight smile to his lips.

"Nothing could be further from the truth, for I like your grandmother very much. And Pen ..." He allowed his voice to trail off, and for the first time since she had met Owen Kendrick Pen thought she detected in him a hesitancy.

She looked up and met his eyes. "Yes, Owen?"

He wavered a moment longer, then gave her hand a small pat. "Nothing. I shall leave you to select your book." He moved away to open the door and paused there. "Pen, I ..."

"Yes?"

He was staring at her, a telltale frown of concentration creasing his brow. Her gaze remained steady as she watched him curiously. He quickly discarded whatever he had been about to say, and abruptly left the room.

Pen waited only long enough to hear his steps recede down the passageway before she set off for the east wing. Owen's tale of his father's death had worked powerfully on her emotions, and she now nursed a strong suspicion that the man responsible for Mr. Kendrick's demise was at that very moment comfortably ensconced in one of the estate's better, albeit dustier, bedchambers.

She rapped on the door and entered without waiting for a reply. James was awake and standing by the window that looked out over the south garden. He was dressed in breeches and a shirt borrowed from Tom that was open at his throat. He turned when she entered and held a hand out to her. "Ah, my little brown wren. I have been waiting to talk with you."

"And I have something to say to you, too, sir! I want those bonds you stole."

He frowned. "Don't you want to ask how my shoulder is feeling?"

"No, I do not! I want you to tell me about the bearer bonds you stole from Owen's father. I have come to take them back."

"Calm yourself, my little wren," he said coaxingly, as he took her hand and led her toward the window. "What has occurred to upset you so?"

"You robbed Owen's father," she accused hotly. "You stopped him less than three miles up the Brighton Road from here, and left him by the road to die."

James plied his mind against the memory of his many victims over the years. "I think I recall that man. He was not as plump in his pockets as I had judged he would be. I got from him only some jewels and a bit of cash and a sheaf of worthless paper."

"Worthless? How can you say such a thing when those bonds are worth a fortune!"

He looked at her sharply. "Are they? Are you certain of that?"

"Don't be ridiculous! You had merely to read them to know their value."

"But therein lies the problem, my dear. Boys of my station in life are not sent to school, but to work. I never learned to read."

That admission took a good deal of the angry wind from Pen's sails. She said, in a much calmer tone, "I beg your pardon. Indeed, how could I have known? Some day I shall tell you how sorry I am for your circumstance. But right now, I need those bonds."

He looked out the window. "I haven't got them."

"Why not? What did you do with them?"

"They were worthless pieces of paper to me. I thought they were nothing but garbage. I didn't keep them."

Pen let loose a moan and sank down onto a nearby chair. "How could you?" she asked, rather pitifully. "How *could* you, James?"

"I didn't know the papers had any value, I assure you."

"No, I'm not talking only about the bonds, I'm talking about everything that—don't you understand that because of you Owen's father died? Don't you feel the least bit responsible?"

"He was alive when I left him," he answered simply, as if that alone should satisfy her.

It did not, of course, and Pen was deeply troubled to learn that the man about whom she had for weeks harbored a romantic crush should be the very same man who might prove to be the ultimate ruin of her family.

"If you haven't the bonds, you must give me something else instead," she said, determined to somehow see some good come from James's rash actions. "Give me something of value that can be pawned for a good deal of money."

"And what will you do with so much money?"

"I shall use it to make someone happy," she answered, and thrust her hand out expectantly.

For a moment she thought he meant to argue with her—or at the very least, protest—but he didn't. Slowly James drew a ring from his finger and placed it in her hand. It was a man's ring, fashioned around a large emerald with diamonds beside it. It did indeed look very costly, and Pen couldn't help wondering if it was the possession of yet another man who had suffered at the hands of The Black Bard.

"Take it," he said. "I had it off some local gentleman who, I assure you, remains to this day alive and well."

"Is that all you have to say?" she asked, feeling a keen sense of disgust mixed with regret. "Have you nothing to offer? No apology to make?"

"My little brown wren, you have much to learn about the ways of the world, and for that I am sorry. I make no other apologies to you."

Those were hardly the words of contrition she had hoped he would utter. For the first time since having made the acquaintance of The Black Bard, Pen could not bring herself to remain in his presence. She slipped the ring into the pocket of her skirt and bade him a hasty good-bye.

In the main hall of the house she found Owen, who was preparing to drive into Brighton.

"Please, may I go with you?" she asked. "Grandmama has asked me to write to my aunt Jane, and I find I am out of writing paper." That excuse for going to Town was, she assured herself, nothing but the truth, but she could not suppress a twinge of guilt over the ring hidden away in her dress pocket.

Owen agreed to wait for her to fetch her gloves and bonnet, and before long they were riding side by side in Owen's curricle toward Brighton. It wasn't until they achieved the edge of Town that she realized she had committed a strategic error, for she could not very well pawn the ring James had given her while in Owen's company.

She asked in what she hoped was a casual tone, "Do you go into Town on business, cousin?"

"Your grandmother has merely commissioned me to perform one or two errands. Altogether, they shall not take long, I think."

"If you wish, you may drop me at the shops and call for me later," suggested Pen.

"And leave you unescorted in Brighton? Certainly not. I shall accompany you wherever you wish to go."

"And what shall I do while you perform Grandmama's errands?"

He looked down at her, his brows flying. "I suppose you shall have to go with me."

"I could do that, but if you were to merely escort me inside whatever shop is most likely to offer the best selection of writing papers, I shall content myself to wait there until you return."

Owen gave the suggestion some consideration, and when it seemed to Pen that he was taking an inordinate amount of time in agreeing with her, she said, "I daresay, that way we shall accomplish our errands much faster."

"I suppose there can be no harm in it," he said as he drew his curricle up in front of a very stylish shop. His tiger leapt down to hold the horses as Owen assisted Pen to the ground. He escorted her into the shop, where she immediately began pointing out to him the various displays of goods that caught her eye.

"Pen, I think it would be wise for me to remain with you."

"If you like you may do so, of course. But I assure you, I could spend hours examining every treasure the store contains. I shall be quite content to remain here if you would like to perform Grandmama's errands."

He hesitated only slightly. "Are you certain you will not be uncomfortable?"

"Not at all!"

"Very well. I should like to get back to Rosemount as soon as possible. I'll see to your grandmother's purchases, and will call here for you as soon as I am finished."

For a moment she was afraid he would see the expression of relief on her face, but he took his leave and she watched through the shop window as he climbed up into his curricle and set off down the street.

She quickly selected a box of writing papers and paid the clerk for them, but when the clerk asked if he could be of any other service to her, she replied that he could, indeed.

"I should like to know if there is a jewelry store nearby of good reputation."

"There is, indeed, miss, right across the street. They have an excellent reputation and a distinguished list of customers."

Pen thanked him kindly, promised to return shortly to collect her writing paper, and left the shop to make her way across the street. The jewelry store was virtually empty when she entered, save for the proprietor and one gentleman customer who stood facing a mirror at the rear of the store as he tried on stickpins.

She approached the counter and asked most politely if she was speaking to the owner.

"You are, indeed, madam," said the man behind the counter. "How may I help you?"

"I should like to sell a piece of jewelry, and I wonder if you would be good enough to tell me if it is a piece you would be interested in purchasing."

She withdrew the ring from her pocket and placed it upon the counter. She saw the jeweler's eyes widen perceptively at the sight of it, and she asked, "Tell me, do you think it is of value?"

"I do, indeed, madam. May I inquire how you came by the ring?"

She hadn't expected such a question, and said, quickly, "It was given to me by a friend."

"I see. Someone very close to you?"

"Oh, yes! Why, we are practically related! He said it was valuable and would fetch a good price, if I ever wished to sell it."

The jeweler fixed her with a hard look, as if he were committing her features to memory. "Your friend was correct, madam. This is a ring of some value, and quite rare. I have seen only one other like it in all my years. Am I to understand that you wish to sell it?"

"Yes, indeed."

"I see. Then, perhaps we may agree upon a price." The jeweler named a sum that seemed to Pen an exorbitant amount.

"Goodness, is it worth that much?"

"Yes, madam, it is. Are we agreed then, that you shall sell the ring to me for that price?" She nodded vigorously in reply and he said, "If you will kindly wait a moment, I will write out a draft against my bank for the purchase."

"Wait! I do not wish to have a bank draft, I wish to have the money."

"But it is a large sum, madam, one that I am not used to having on hand in my shop."

"Well, how much money *do* you have?" she asked.

He looked a little bit stunned. "Madam, is there someone you might call upon to do your bargaining for you?"

"But we have already struck a bargain, you and I."

"Yes, madam, but usually, people do their best to make me pay more for an item, not less. I should be taking advantage of you if I paid you less than our agreed upon price. Only think of my conscience!"

"Oh, it makes no never mind, for I give you permission to cheat me, if you like. It is very important that I sell the ring for cash, and if that means I shall take less than what you offered, so be it."

"I see," said the jeweler, but he was troubled nevertheless by the direction their bargaining had taken. "Perhaps we can come to an agreement. I shall give you what cash I have, and shall write a draft for the remainder of the price. Does that sound fair?"

"I think that is very fair," she said happily. She was still feeling pleased when at last she left the jeweler's shop with her reticule stuffed with bills and a single bank draft.

The jeweler solicitously escorted her to the door and bowed her through it, but no sooner did he close that same door upon her than he turned to the gentleman who was engaged with stickpins at the looking glass and asked, "Sir, would you be so kind as to look at this ring and see if you recognize it?"

Chapter Ten

Robert Carswell would have known that ring anywhere. There were only two like it in existence. One of them was nestled on a pillow of velvet on the shop counter; the other was on his right hand.

"My father's ring!" he exclaimed.

"Yes, sir. I suspected as much."

"Tell me, where did you get it?"

"A rather extraordinary young lady brought it in just now."

"Lady? Where is she? Where did she go?"

"She is there, sir," said the jeweler, pointing out the window to where Pen was just reaching the other side of the street.

"Pen? Pen Hamilton brought it in?" Robert asked, incredulously.

"Do you know the young lady, sir?"

"I should say I do. Did she tell you how she came by it?"

"She said it was given to her by a friend."

"Did she? Well, if that don't beat—tell me, did she happen to mention the friend's name?"

"No, sir. She was merely interested in selling the ring for cash."

"How the deuce do you suppose she came to have it?" asked Robert, quite stunned by such an odd turn of events. The ring had been stolen years before by that notorious highwayman, The Black Bard, and Robert had despaired of ever seeing it again. It had belonged to his father, and it was the sentimental loss he lamented more than the ring itself. How had Pen Hamilton come into possession of it?

"Perhaps," said the jeweler, "the young lady is acquainted with the man who stole the ring in the first place, sir."

Robert picked up the ring and began to examine it carefully. "That couldn't possibly be true! Egad, man, this ring was stolen by none other than The Black Bard!"

"The young lady did mention that the ring was given to her by a friend," the jeweler reminded him. "She said she was practically related to the man."

Robert ceased his examination of the ring and cast a look of appalled surprise at the jeweler. "Good God! Do you know what this means?"

"No, sir, I do not, but I am hopeful you will discover some truth in all of this."

It was a truth Robert Carswell would rather not face. Try as he might, he could think of no explanation for

Pen having the ring except that she must be in league somehow with The Black Bard. And when he chanced to think who of Pen's acquaintance fit the highwayman's description, an image of his good friend, Owen Kendrick, swam before his eyes. Both men had black hair; both men were of similar height and proportions. Owen was an excellent horseman, as was the Black Bard.

He could hardly bring himself to believe it—indeed, he firmly hoped it wasn't true—but the notion that Owen Kendrick was none other than The Black Bard made perfect sense. He had long known that the Kendrick family was feeling the wind; Owen himself had confessed to Robert that his financial situation was grave, indeed. Yet Robert had also seen, time after time, how Owen had suddenly managed to come up with needed funds at regular intervals—almost as often as The Black Bard staged his Brighton Road robberies.

He tried not to allow that seed of doubt grow. Yet when he chanced to think that Owen—a man he had long considered to be of the highest moral tone and strictest principals—was himself the most notorious highwayman in all of England, he began to feel angry, indeed. What better way to disguise his crimes, thought Robert, than for Owen to hide behind a daytime cloak of respectability?

He was engaged to call upon the Kendrick family the very next evening that they might all attend the prince's ball together, but now he very much doubted he would be able to face Owen. Only the thought that he had to know for certain whether or not his longtime friend was the notorious highwayman caused him to consider keeping that appointment.

Pen was blithely unaware that she had been recognized in the jeweler's shop. In fact, she was feeling very well pleased with herself when at last she and Owen returned home. She found her grandmother in her sitting room, searching the drawers of her dressing table.

"Grandmama, may I come in? I have something for you," she said.

"Only tell me you have my ruby earrings with the diamond drops, and I shall be happy!"

"No, Grandmama, but I have brought—"

"Then help me look for them, my dear. I had wished to wear those earrings tonight, but I cannot find them anywhere!"

"Grandmama, I am certain they shall turn up, but in the meantime I have something very important to give to you." Pen drew her reticule from her arm and pulled from its folds the stack of bills.

"Merciful heavens, child! What is this?"

"It is for you, Grandmama," she said, as she placed the bills in her grandmother's hand. "It is the money to pay for a ball at Rosemount."

Mrs. Kendrick looked at her in astonishment. "But how . . . my dear, where did you come by such a sum?"

"I am sworn to secrecy, so I may not tell you. Please don't tease yourself by asking questions that I will not answer."

"But this is . . . I can scarce believe it!"

"Don't you see, Grandmama? Now you will not have to apply to Owen to host a ball. Now you may pay for it yourself!"

"My dear child, you haven't done anything illegal, have you?"

"No, Grandmama," said Pen with a laugh. "Please take the money. It would make me happy if you did."

Mrs. Kendrick looked down at the stack of bills in her hand as if she could scarce believe it to be true. "I don't know what to say!"

"Say you will ready your cards of invitation. Say you will use this money to host the grandest ball Rosemount has ever seen."

Mrs. Kendrick swallowed hard, and a mist of tears gathered in her eyes. "Dearest girl," she exclaimed as she clasped Pen to her. "Only wait until I have told Augusta! She will be in raptures when I tell her what you have done!"

"Grandmama, you must not tell anyone you had the money from me."

"But why not? I want everyone to know what a dear, *dear* granddaughter you are!"

"No, Grandmama," said Pen sternly. "You must promise me that you shall never speak of this to anyone."

Bewildered yet compliant, Mrs. Kendrick pledged to keep Pen's secret. But there was a noticeable change in her from that moment on. She was, arguably, the happiest she had been in years—so much so that even Peter chanced to remark upon it.

He was coming down the stair the next afternoon as his grandmother and Owen were going up.

"Hello, Grandmother. Owen." He placed a light kiss upon her cheek and said, "That's a very fetching bit of lace upon your head. Is it new?"

"I've worn this cap for years, my dear."

"Well, you look quite charming in it. You've always been a handsome woman, Grandmother, but now that I think on it, you have been in excellent looks these past days. Tell me, what have you done with yourself?"

"Nothing out of the way, I assure you!" she said, with a light laugh. Feeling quite euphoric, she plucked up the courage to say, "Owen and I were just about to drive out to visit my friend, Lady Ambersleigh. Why don't you go with us? She is your godmother, after all, and you haven't seen her in an age."

"I wish I could," he replied with a noticeable lack of sincerity, "but I'm engaged to meet the prince, and I'll be with him all day. Owen, you'll make the pretty for me with my godmother, won't you?"

"I'll give her your regrets," said Owen mildly.

"I knew I could rely on you. Once the prince returns to London I'll be able to squire you about a bit more, Grandmother. At least, until I remove to London, too. He has his mind made up to buy Lord Grayson's bays—all four of them!—but said he would wait until I had a chance to look at them for him."

Owen frowned. "Peter, I think you should reconsider—"

"I know what you're going to say—stay away from Grayson's stables. His horses may look like sweet goers from afar but, like you, I've heard rumors the nags are winded before they've even left their blocks."

Mrs. Kendrick resumed her ascent to the next floor, saying, "Then I shall not see you again today, I think, Peter. When you see the prince, if he should ask about your family, I hope you will tell him how humbled we are to have received his invitation."

"Of course, Grandmother, but we don't wish to appear *too* humble, now do we?" he returned with a laugh.

Mrs. Kendrick disappeared down an upper passageway and Peter resumed his progress down the stairs. He hadn't taken many more steps when Owen leaned over the banisters and said commandingly, "Peter!" That young man looked up, a question in his eyes. "I need a word with you, if you please."

"But I'm on my way out. The prince is waiting on me."

"This will only take a moment." Owen went down the remaining stairs with Peter to the library, and held the door open meaningfully.

Peter passed into the room with a grudging expression, and when Owen nodded toward a chair he said in a sullen tone, "One day, cousin, you will find you are no longer able to order me about!"

Owen serenely accepted this stricture. "I shall look forward to the day. In the meantime, I wish to speak to you about something."

"Very well!" he said with little grace. "What is it this time?"

"Your plan to remove to London. I'm afraid, Peter,

you will need to reconsider the trip. The London town house is no longer available to you.''

Peter was on his feet in an instant, saying furiously, "First you cut off my credit, and now this! I . . . I won't stand for it, do you hear me? Of all the shabby tricks!''

"There is no trick, Peter,'' said Owen calmly.

"Isn't there? It seems to me you take a great delight in denying my family and me the simplest of pleasures! Tyranny doesn't become you, cousin!''

For the barest of moments Owen was sorely tempted to return a stinging answer, but he controlled himself and walked over to where the portrait of his father hung on the wall beside the desk. After a pause, he said, somewhat ruthlessly, "The London house is gone. Sold. It is no longer a property of the Kendrick family.''

Surprised, Peter sputtered, "But . . . but I was just there, not above three weeks ago!''

"I know. I was in London at the same time, although not in the same house as you. I completed the sale just before I returned here to Rosemount.''

Peter gave his head a slight shake. "But, *why?* Why in God's name would you do such a thing?''

"Because our family is about to go wading into the River Tick.''

There was a stunned silence. "Good God, do you mean to tell me we are broke? Lord, Owen, this isn't some sort of cruel hoax of yours, is it?''

Owen gave a short laugh. "I think you know that my sense of humor doesn't run in that vein.''

"But how can this be? You've been a veritable martinet with us all, begrudging us anything new, and handing us shillings and telling us to call them pounds! Ever since your father died you've been tight-fisted in the extreme.''

''I had hoped simple economies would save us. I was wrong,'' he said simply.

Peter sank slowly back onto his chair and asked in a stunned tone, ''How the devil could such a thing happen?''

Owen told him about the bonds his father had carried with him the night he was robbed on the Brighton Road.

''Do you mean to tell me that all this time you've been staving off creditors?'' Peter asked. ''And all this time, I've been buying new suits of clothes, gambling deep, and entertaining friends? And then there was Augusta's season, which must have cost the earth, and—!'' He stopped short and cast an accusing look at Owen. ''You should have told me!''

Owen shook his head. ''Only one other person— a friend, let us say—knows the entire story.''

''You told a friend before you told your family?'' demanded Peter incredulously.

''I had a responsibility, and I think my father would have wanted me to do my best to provide for you and your family before I cried defeat.''

Peter stood and took a turn about the room. He stopped after a moment and cast a frowning look at Owen. ''You've got more pride than Wellington's troops! Dash it, I know you and I are not blood rela-ions, but we *are* family! You should have told me. I could have helped, you know.''

"Perhaps, although I don't know how," said Owen simply.

"I could have stepped back a bit from my friendship with the prince, for one thing. That is an association that has a dear price tag attached to it, I can tell you!"

"You'll oblige me by maintaining that particular friendship a while longer," said Owen sternly, although he was feeling a little touched by Peter's willingness to help. "The prince's ball is one of the few things your grandmother and sister have had to look forward to in some time. I won't deny them the treat."

Peter frowned again. "You have to tell them."

"Not yet."

"Owen, they think you are dicing pennies merely because you are mean-spirited."

"I know."

"But they must be told! You cannot wish them to think ill of you when you have done your best all this time to keep us all afloat! God knows I haven't treated you fairly!"

"I shall tell them after the ball. There is no good in dampening their enjoyment of it, for if things continue on their present course the ball at The Pavilion shall be the last entertainment they will attend for some time to come."

"Will you lose Rosemount, then?"

Owen felt a sudden tightening in his throat, but he managed to say with perfect calm, "That is an excellent possibility."

"God, I am sorry, Owen! If only I had a tenth now

of all the money I left at the faro table—! But there is no use dwelling on that, I suppose."

"No, there isn't," said Owen. There was not the least trace of censure in his tone, a fact that Peter observed gratefully.

"Listen, I do have to leave now. After all, a fellow cannot keep his future king waiting. But when I return I want the rest of the news, and no cream on it, if you please. I know I've never given you any reason to think I'm anything more than just fancy shoes and waistcoats, but you should have trusted me."

"Yes. You are right, of course."

"I'm glad you agree, for I don't mean to be kept any longer in the dark over this," said Peter with determination. "God, when I think of all the times I cursed you for tightening my funds and cutting my allowance—! I think I could kill you if I didn't feel such charity for you!"

He left the room after a few minutes to keep his appointment with the prince. Peter's feeling of good will toward Owen and the rest of the family prevailed, and when the day of the prince's ball arrived, he announced that he would attend that august function with his family and personally ensure that they all gained the prince's notice. He had even taken steps, he said, to ensure that Robert Carswell joined their party to even out their number.

They were all to assemble in the drawing room prior to boarding the carriage that would take them to The Pavilion. Wishing to have time to make a quick pilgrimage to the east wing to visit with James before leaving for the evening, Pen dressed early. She stepped carefully into the rose-colored dress and sat, somewhat impatiently, as Betty arranged the laces about her slim shoulders and set her hair in a mass of glowing curls about the top of her head. When at last Betty was finished and she waved Pen over to stand in front of the pier glass hung in one corner of her room, Pen was astonished by the reflection she saw there. She had never thought herself a beauty, but she could not have been more pleased with her appearance. The gown fitted her perfectly, and its color lent a faint blush of color to her complexion and a glow to her vivid brown eyes. She wondered what Owen's reaction would be when he saw her, and if he would think she was pretty.

That James thought her attractive, she could not doubt. His eyes lit appreciatively when she entered his room. He went to her immediately, and took her hands in his. "What a vision you are, dear little wren. You are even more lovely than ever, if that is possible."

She found herself being led farther into the room, past items of furniture that had not been there before, along with an assortment of trunks, valises, and boxes of varying shapes and sizes. "Where did all this come from?"

"These are my possessions."

"But why did you bring them here?"

"I couldn't very well leave them unattended out there," said James with a wave of his hand in the general direction of the window. He smiled slightly "What if someone were to steal them?"

That smile—which Pen might have counted as charming a few days ago—now appeared to be little more than cheeky. She said, with a hint of censure, "You are supposed to be getting well so that you may *leave*. It appears instead as if you have moved in."

"Would you mind so very much if I did?" he asked, raising one of her hands toward his lips.

She felt an urgent need to snatch her fingers from within his grasp, but she waited until he had fulfilled his gallant gesture before she withdrew her hand from his. "I wish you would not do that, sir."

"You didn't mind when I did it before," he reminded her. "Tell me, why are you looking even more lovely than usual this evening?"

"I am attending a ball tonight. Indeed, the entire family will be there, so you may rest easy and not be afraid of detection."

"I very rarely worry about such things. I move as quietly as a cat, you know. In fact, I could have those earrings from your ears before you ever suspected what I was about."

"I wish you wouldn't speak such nonsense," she said crossly.

"Shall I tell you instead how enchanting you look tonight?"

"No. You shall merely promise to be good and stay in your room until I get back!"

He laughed then, a circumstance which Pen found most irritating. She left him and would have slammed the door at her departure had she not feared that someone in the household might hear her do so.

Back in Pen's room, Betty placed an evening cloak about her shoulders and Pen went downstairs to find that Robert Carswell had arrived and the carriage was at the door.

"Six people in one carriage shall be a tight fit," remarked Owen, "but I daresay we shall manage. You don't mind, do you, Carswell?"

"Not at all," said that gentleman with perfect equanimity, but his eyes strayed toward Augusta and lingered there for a moment before he offered her his arm in escort.

They rode to The Pavilion in relative silence, broken only by a brief conversation in which Mrs. Kendrick complimented Augusta on her choice of jewels.

"These?" asked Augusta, fingering the short string of pearls at her neck. "I had meant to wear my amethyst brooch instead, but it has gone missing, I'm afraid. I can't imagine where I might have left it, and I'm convinced it must be in my room somewhere. I have set my maid to the task of finding it, but in the meantime I must be content, I suppose, to wear my pearls."

"It looks as though we have both grown forgetful, my dear," said Mrs. Kendrick, "for I have misplaced my ruby earrings. I am certain they shall turn up somewhere!"

In the dim light of the carriage, Robert cast a probing look across to where Pen and Owen were sitting side by side. "That is a very odd coincidence. Don't you think that odd, Miss Hamilton?"

It seemed to Pen that the only thing odd was Robert Carswell's question, but she said quite simply, "It is a fantastic coincidence, indeed. If you like, Augusta

I shall be glad to help you look for your brooch once we are returned home.''

"We shall all help look for the brooch, if you like,'' said her grandmother happily, "although I am certain it shall be found bye and bye!''

Their carriage approached The Pavilion, and Pen resisted an impulse to hang her head out the carriage window in order to have a clear and unobstructed view of the place. She longed to see if all the many fantastic stories she had heard about The Pavilion and its design were true. On her forays into Town she had seen the onion-shaped domes of The Pavilion rising above the tops of the trees from a distance, and she had thought it must be an elegant place of magical character.

As their carriage made its way down the drive and circled its way toward the main entrance, she did not think she would have to amend that opinion. Certainly, The Pavilion was much larger than she had ever envisioned, and when she stepped across the threshold and entered the octagonal hall she was delighted by what she found there.

The entrance hall had about it the feel of a charming garden pavilion, with a high ceiling that had been plastered to convey the effect of a tent drapery. The room was exquisitely furnished, and large windows that spanned floor-to-ceiling rendered views of the lawns and flower beds.

In an anteroom, the ladies left off their cloaks, and as they emerged to rejoin the gentlemen Pen found that Owen's gaze had settled appreciatively upon her.

"So that is the gown you told me about,'' he said

in a soft voice. "You neglected to confess to me how lovely you look in it."

That was the compliment she had hoped to receive, but she had not been prepared for the series of blushes that threatened to creep up her neck. He offered her his arm then, and smiled down upon her as she tentatively placed her hand on his.

Peter led them into the next room, where the Prince Regent was receiving his guests, and Pen found that the excitement she had felt over meeting a member of the royal family was quickly vanquished at first sight of him. She had seen portraits of him over the years, and while she had to admit they did him justice she found she could not admire the man in person. He had about him, she thought, a look of excess that was in perfect keeping with the royal residence. His face was rather florid and he was, she judged, overweight. When he nodded a greeting to them all she could have sworn she heard his stays creak. He was, however, very attentive toward them all, a fact which greatly gratified Mrs. Kendrick and caused Peter to smile with satisfaction. She noticed that when Owen came to stand before him, the Prince Regent clasped Owen's hand between both of his and greeted him warmly.

They passed on into the next room, and then another, each one more magnificent than the last. When they entered the music room where the dancing would be held, Pen gasped softly and stared in astonishment at the decorations and appointments.

She hardly knew whether to be intrigued or repulsed by the sight. Everywhere she looked were images of vicious, winged dragons and enormous snakes, writhing and twisting along the ceiling cove and hanging from the enormous chandeliers. There were Chinese pagodas that almost traveled the height of the ceiling before each window in the room, and everywhere she looked she saw silk draperies of vibrant colors and elaborate carvings of costly woods. Even the mantelpiece was remarkable. Made of marble and ormolu, it was a massive, columned structure that stretched well above their heads.

"What do you think, Pen?" asked Owen.

"I hope I have assumed correctly that all of the snakes in this room are not, in fact, real."

He laughed. "I believe you are safe to enter."

"It is all rather overpowering, though, isn't it? I cannot be sure I like it very much."

"Then you and I are agreed on this subject, at least."

"Nonsense! You and I have agreed countless times before!"

"Have we?" he asked, cocking one dark brow in question. "Now, why don't I remember that? Come, let me show you some of the other rooms."

Pen found herself being led away from the others and asked in surprise, "Have you been here to The Pavilion before?"

"Once or twice. Peter is not the only one who can claim an acquaintance with the regent."

"So that is why the prince greeted you so generously! I wondered over it, but never dreamed you shared a friendship with him. Why have you never said anything before?"

"Let us merely say that my relationship with the prince is not one of deep feeling. We were rather close once, years ago, but our paths and our sensibilities took different directions, you might say."

They had by this time entered an adjoining room. A long gallery with floor-to-ceiling windows down the entire length of one wall, it was a richly appointed room with Chinese paintings in heavy gold frames, gilt panels, and heavy silk curtains and upholstery. Through the open door Pen could see the guests in the music room beyond, but in the gallery she and Owen were quite alone. This gave her the courage to say, "What a mystery you are, Owen Kendrick! What pleasure do you get from being so secretive about yourself?"

He looked down at her with a mild question in his eyes. "I haven't any secrets—at least, I have none from you."

She gave her head a small shake of wonder. "Every time I think I am beginning to know you well, you say or do something that convinces me that I know you not at all. I told you once that you were not the man you first appeared to be. Little did I know how quickly my words would prove to be true!"

He placed his own hand over her fingers, still nestled in the crook of his elbow. "I never tried to deceive you about myself. I told you I had a temper, and I do. I have always been honest with you, as you have been with me."

Of all the words he might have chosen to say at that very moment, none could have caused Pen more distress. For no sooner did she look up into his eyes than a flushing wave of guilt swept over her. She struggled against a sudden impulse to confess to Owen that the source of all his troubles had set up housekeeping in one of his own spare bedrooms. Her fingers fluttered against his arm, and she quickly averted her eyes, saying nervously, "Did I just now hear the music begin? Should we not go back in with the others?"

"I did promise to lead you out for the first dance, didn't I?" he asked as he ushered back over to where the rest of the family had gathered.

"Where did you two run off to?" asked Robert, running a suspicious glance over both of them.

"Pen wished to see some of the other rooms before they became too filled with guests to be appreciated."

Robert frowned. "And did you find anything? Anything that struck your fancy?"

"I believe Pen has a mind to take one or two of the gilt snakes home with her," answered Owen with such perfect composure that Pen couldn't help but smile.

Robert was not as amused, and he said most earnestly, "Owen, as a friend, is there anything you would like to tell me? Anything in particular you wish to discuss with me?"

"No, but now that you mention it I would appreciate it if you would lead Augusta out for the first dance," Owen replied as the orchestra struck the opening chords of the first set. "I, you see, have promised this dance to Pen."

As on the one other occasion she had danced with Owen, Pen now found him to be a graceful and attentive partner. She also found herself looking upon him as the most attractive man of her acquaintance; certainly, he was a finer gentleman than The Black Bard. That man, she had come to realize, was not quite so heroic and romantic a figure once he came down off his horse.

Except for remarking upon her fine eyes and commenting upon the kissable state of her lips, she had discovered that The Black Bard hadn't any conversation at all. She had once thought him a kind of Robin Hood figure, who—she had been certain—used his booty for some noble cause such as helping the poor. She had discovered, though, that he was content to merely squander whatever he stole. She was vastly disappointed in him and found him to be lacking, indeed, when compared to Owen Kendrick.

In Owen she saw a man of principle and honor, a man to be admired for having taken on the enormous responsibilities of his family and estates. That feeling she had once counted as tenderness toward him swelled slightly into a more substantial emotion.

She looked over to where Robert and Augusta had joined the set and saw that Robert had abandoned his suspicious glances in their direction for the more fulfilling prospect of gazing into Augusta's eyes. "You have made two people very happy tonight, I think."

"So you have noticed that, too? I didn't think anyone else was aware that Robert and Augusta were in love."

She almost missed a step. "You know?" she asked in surprise.

"Certainly. Why do you think I allow Robert to

haunt Rosemount, if not to give him plenty of opportunity to at last declare himself?''

"But why would you wish him to do that?"

He laughed slightly. "So that he and Augusta may
at last be married. Why else would I encourage him
to make a cake of himself?"

The movement of the dance caused them to sepa-
rate for a few moments, and when they at last came
back together Pen blurted, "But I thought you wished
Augusta to marry another. I thought that was why last
year you sent her to London for the season."

"I didn't send her, but I did allow her to go. It was
your grandmother's idea that Augusta should make
her curtsies. I was opposed to the idea at first, but your
grandmother convinced me she should be allowed to
go, and after a while I agreed. I thought that if she
attended all the parties and balls in London, she
would be content then to come home to Rosemount
and marry Robert."

"But she didn't marry Robert."

"I know, and for the life of me I cannot understand
what happened. I never asked, and I didn't think it
my place to pry."

"So you never intended for Augusta to find a husband in London?"

"Why would I, when she was already in love with
Robert, and he with her?"

"But this is marvelous news!" exclaimed Pen. "I
am so glad we had this conversation."

"In that case, so am I, although I'm not at all sure
I understand why."

She laughed then. "Tell them they have your blessing."

"Unnecessary! Augusta knows I shall gladly approve a match with Robert."

"I am certain she must think so, but that is not the same as hearing it from your own lips. Please, will you do it? It will make both of them so very happy."

He looked down at her for a long moment "Will it make you happy, too?"

"It will, indeed!"

"Then I shall do it," he said, emphatically.

Their dance ended and Owen escorted Pen back to her grandmother, who immediately complimented them both on their fine skill on the dance floor. "You must make it a habit to practice your steps together," she said, "for I am counting on you to lead out the first dance at my ball, as well. We shall show everyone that the Kendricks of Rosemount can host just as grand a party as the Prince Regent himself!"

Chapter Eleven

Owen Kendrick sat in his favorite chair in the darkened library, a cigar in one hand and a glass of brandy in the other, and wondered what on earth he was going to do about Pen Hamilton.

It was in his nature to be intrigued by contradiction, and he had learned almost the moment of their acquaintance that Pen was a young woman of contrasts. He had found her to be at once innocent and fun-loving, optimistic and infuriating, good-natured and stubborn. He had, however, never thought her dishonest. Until now.

At first, he had suspected nothing amiss. A lost pair of earrings, a misplaced brooch, his own gold pen taken from its casing—these he had discounted as minor accidents or the products of a forgetful memory. Even when he had come to realize that trinkets and treasures were going missing from rooms all over the house, he had no more than suspected the servants of the crime. Then he chanced to recall that his servants were all employees of long standing, and that pilfering and petty theft had never been a problem on the estate—until Miss Pen Hamilton's arrival. He realized he had no choice but to believe the worst. Pen was a thief.

He could not have been more disappointed in her. In Pen he had begun to think he had at last made the acquaintance of someone who was guileless and genuine; someone who didn't make up to him simply because he held the purse strings in the family. Unlike Mrs. Kendrick and Augusta, and—especially—Peter, Pen had never asked him for a thing, had never made a demand on him. Now he knew why. She didn't need his money because she had her own—money she had stolen from her own household, her own family.

Almost he wished he did not know Pen's secret; almost he wished Mrs. Kendrick had never naively uttered those fateful words in the music room of The Pavilion. But in her happiness over the betrothal of Augusta and Robert she had blurted out the news that she was planning to hold a ball at Rosemount, a ball he had expressly forbidden her to host.

He had waited until the evening was over to confront her about the remark, and Mrs. Kendrick, never a match against a will stronger than her own, had quickly admitted that the whole thing had been Pen's idea. Where *had* she got the money, he wondered, and then he chanced to recall all the many items that had gone missing.

He had no choice but to think the worst of her, but he was hopeful that by consuming a good portion of a brandy bottle he might not be obliged to think of her often. He hoped the alcoholic fumes that reduced his brain to a slightly fuddled state might erase the memory of her wide, brown eyes, the softness of her skin beneath his fingers, and the manner in which her hair formed a fetching frame about her lovely face. But on this night, even the alcohol failed him. Try as he might, he could not banish from his mind the image of Pen Hamilton in his arms.

He poured the last of the brandy into his glass and drank it down in a single motion. Ignoring the temptation to hurl the glass against the fireplace, he set it back down on the table with a snap and left the library to make his way up to his own apartment. It was very late, and all the candles in the hall had been extinguished.

The vast front hall and staircase were dark, but he didn't care. He could find his way around his beloved Rosemount with his eyes closed, and though his eyes were open, they were certainly blurry from the amount of brandy he had consumed. He was just about to climb the staircase when he saw a light above him. Someone carrying a candle was on the next landing.

Owen took to the stairs and reached the landing just in time to see the candle disappear around a corner. He thought he had detected a glimpse of a white gown in the fast-fading light of the candle. Irritated, curious, and most of all, angry, he followed the waning candlelight and found that he was making his way in the direction of his own apartments.

Another turn in the passageway and he had a full view of the specter moving quietly past the door to his rooms. It was Pen, clad only in a nightdress and wrapper. She was carrying a candle in one hand and a tray of some kind in another, and she was clearly on her way to the east wing.

A deep sense of outrage overwhelmed him. All the feelings of betrayal and disappointment he had been feeling came to the fore. Before he considered his actions, before he took a moment to decide what he would say, he found himself sprinting across the floor to where Pen was opening the passage door that led to the east wing.

He captured her there in the darkened hallway, grabbing the candle from her with one hand and seizing her shoulder with the other. She let out a scream of fright, and the tray she had been carrying clattered to the floor.

"What are you doing?" he demanded. "Tell me! What business have you in the east wing that I should continually find you here?"

Pen didn't think her heart would ever recover from the shock he had given her, but she was more concerned about the vise-like grip he had locked upon her shoulder. "Owen, you are hurting me!"

"Not as much as you have hurt me, my girl. To think I actually trusted you! To think I confided in you!"

Anger and a deep sense of mortification overcame him. There, standing before him, already within his grasp, was the one person he held responsible for such emotions. Before he knew it, before he even realized his own intentions, he had caught her in a crushing embrace.

"Admit it!" he commanded through clenched teeth. "Admit that you are nothing but a thief who preys upon and makes victims of her own family!"

Pen tried to speak, tried desperately to deny the allegations, but found she was capable of emitting little more than a gasp of fright. How he had discovered that she had secreted the highwayman away in the house, she could not guess. She knew only that he was inordinately angry—much more angry than she had ever dreamed he would be—and he had apparently assumed that she was somehow in league with the robber.

He looked down upon her through narrowed eyes. "Say something. *Say* something! God, what a fool I have been! To think that I had actually started believe I was a little bit in love with you."

Then, before he even knew his own intentions, he was kissing her, so ruthlessly that she struggled desperately to free herself. Her efforts had no more effect than the wings of a butterfly fluttering against his chest. Even with only one arm about her, he was able to hold her securely against him.

Pen couldn't get away and she couldn't make him stop. She could only hope that if she succumbed to his kisses, he might let her go.

No sooner did her struggles cease than the tenor of his kiss changed. Gone was the bruising pressure of his mouth against hers. Instead, his lips softened and seemed to coax from hers a response that was very near a piercing sweetness. His arm, still holding her securely against him, moved slightly, and his hand snaked down her back. She gave a little gasp, and every inch of her body suddenly realized a kind of heightened sensitivity.

She could have sworn she felt his heart beat against her breast, underscoring the intimacy of their embrace. Her own heart, she thought bitterly, could never be trusted again, for it chose that moment to betray her. No longer did she consider that his kiss was some kind of punishment; no longer did she fear the feeling of the length of his body pressed hard against her own. In spite of herself, she felt herself responding to his kiss.

His lips kissed and teased hers, leaving her feeling breathless and exhilarated and desperate to have him kiss her yet again. Just as she began to wish that his kiss would go on forever, that they might remain in each others' arms for the rest of their lives, he raised his head.

He released her then, as abruptly as he had first captured her. As if he wished to put some distance between them, he stepped a little away. He still held the candle, but with his other hand he ran his fingers through his hair in an exasperated fashion.

"Pen, I will give you just one more chance to tell me what you have done with the things you have stolen."

She felt as if her heart had risen into her throat. "Owen, I haven't stolen anything. I swear to you, I am speaking the truth!"

"Then what were you doing just now, prowling about the house and sneaking into the east wing?"

"Owen, I . . . I—!"

She stopped short, unwilling to lie and unable to tell him the truth. She had just witnessed his anger when he thought her nothing more than a petty thief. How much more furious he would be to discover that she was guilty of a far worse crime! To think her responsible for purloining trinkets was one thing. If he were to discover that she had hidden his nemesis under his very own roof, he might never forgive her.

"For God's sake, Pen, say *some*thing!" he commanded.

"I cannot tell you anything, so please don't ask me again!"

"I don't have to ask, for I think I already have a good idea of your character," he said angrily. "You've been stealing from this house and hiding your treasures in the east wing."

"I . . . I haven't!" she protested.

"Don't deny it, for I find myself hard-pressed to believe anything you may say."

"But I am speaking the truth! Owen, I have done nothing to make you suspect me of stealing."

"No? Then where did you get the money to give to your grandmother? How did you come by the funds to hold a ball at Rosemount?" He saw a telltale flush cover her cheeks. "You didn't think I'd know. I see. You thought you would buy your grandmother's silence, and I would never know what you had done. You must think me the greatest of fools!"

She tried to speak, but succeeded in emitting only a small sob.

He watched her a moment, frowning, his expression very solemn indeed in the shadowy light of the candle. His jaw tightened perceptibly, and he took a step toward her. For one brief, dizzying, terrifying moment, she thought he meant to take her in his arms again, and she didn't know whether to be glad or alarmed. But instead of once again clasping her to him, he grasped her hand and thrust the candlestick between her fingers.

"Take this. Take it and go to bed, Pen," he said, in a voice that sounded as if he carried the weight of the world on his shoulders.

She didn't have to be asked a second time. Close to tears, she hurried off to her own bedchamber, keenly aware that her legs and arms had started to tremble rather violently.

She didn't see Owen again for several days. With the memory of his behavior in the passageway still fresh upon her mind and the feel of his punishing lips against hers still indelibly etched upon her lips, she knew she could not face him. She refused to go to the stables in the mornings as she had been used to. When she realized that he was absenting himself throughout the remainder of the day and declining, with one excuse or another, to take his meals with the family, she was forced to admit to herself that he was just as studiously avoiding her presence.

That was a loss she felt keenly, for she was now thoroughly convinced that she was hopelessly and completely in love with Owen. Whatever feelings whatever emotions, she had believed herself to know for The Black Bard were nothing compared to the affection she now had for Owen. She missed him dreadfully, and longed for their times together. Even more did she miss the trust Owen had placed in her, and no amount of tears in the world, she realized, could ever make Owen trust her again.

Chapter Twelve

Pen avoided going to the east wing in the evenings unless she was certain Owen was away from the house. She didn't feel she could risk another confrontation with him any more than she could stand to see the unspoken accusations reflected in his eyes when they settled upon her.

She limited her visits with James only during the daylight hours. Even these meetings, which had once been the highlight of her days, had deteriorated into little more than chores. Each day she saw James's health improve, and each day she noticed more trunks and chests collected in his room.

"These things weren't here before," she said, noticing a porcelain box encrusted with jewels on a nearby tabletop. "Where did this come from?"

"Where do *all* my things come from?" asked James

with his smile that now held none of its previous charm for her.

"But you had none of these things when last I was in this room. How did they get here?"

"I felt this room was in need of decoration. It was much too plain, too solemn a place for a man of my tastes."

She had a sudden thought, and hoped with all her being that her suspicions were wrong. "You haven't been going out, have you? Tell me you have not been robbing travelers while you have been staying here at Rosemount!"

"Of course I have," he said with perfect calm. "I must, after all, do what I can to make my poor living."

Pen felt a rush of panic. "But—but you have turned Rosemount into your—your hideout!"

"Ingenious of me, wasn't it? I did what I could to make the best of a bad situation, and I think I have done quite well by myself."

"But not by me! You seem to forget this is not my home. Rosemount belongs to the Kendricks, an old and respected family!"

"Exactly! And what better place to hide myself and my booty than under the very nose of the most priggish man in all of England!"

"You are wrong!" she retorted, deeply wounded. "Owen Kendrick is a fine man of honor and feeling, and—and you would do well to emulate him!"

"Don't fret, my little puritan," said James with a laugh as he took her in his arms. "I won't harm your precious Mr. Kendrick."

He didn't try to kiss her, a fact which Pen found

to be a great relief, but he did insist upon holding her a moment and remarking upon the softness of her skin.

"I would wish that you not speak to me so!" she said, struggling out of his arms with little effort.

"Shall I tell you instead how much I have missed the sweet taste of your lips?"

"No, but you might tell me how quickly you can remove yourself and your ill-gotten gains!"

He laughed again. "My, you are a passionate one!"

Pen drew herself up to her full height and said with as much dignity as she could muster, "I shall have Tom Hawkins see to your arm. Since it seems to be sufficiently healed that you may go out robbing people, I assume it is sufficiently healed that you may leave this house!"

"In good time," he said, quite unperturbed by her outburst. "Everything happens in good time, my little brown wren."

It seemed to Pen that her life had turned to rubble on all fronts. When she had first arrived, she had so wanted to make everyone at Rosemount happy. Instead, she had succeeded in causing those she loved the utmost grief.

Only Mrs. Kendrick seemed truly glad for Pen's company, and she made it a habit whenever she found herself alone with Pen to thank her once again for having used her clever wits to find the means of financing the ball. She begged Pen's assistance in the endeavor, and—in part to please her grandmother, in part to take her mind off of Owen and that horrid highwayman tucked away in the east wing—Pen threw herself into helping with the preparations.

Pen could scarcely bring herself to step inside the east wing of the house, so loathsome did she find the company of The Black Bard. So it was a bit ironic that she found herself charged with overseeing the household servants as they aired out the gallery and the ballroom and made those rooms ready for the ball.

It was up to Pen to ensure that the floors were buffed, the chandeliers cleaned, and the panels dusted and polished. She helped select the dinner menu and consulted with the gardener as to the proper arrangements of flowers to grace the tables in both rooms.

As the appointed day neared, there were a hundred small details that commanded her attention, yet all the activity in the world could not make her forget the ache in her heart. She knew she would see Owen at the ball, for Mrs. Kendrick had mentioned that he had pledged to be there, as had dear Mr. Carswell.

"I am counting on them, you know," she said as she once again went over the guest list with Pen. "I am hopeful Owen will dance the first dance with you again, just as he did at the regent's ball. Such a fine and graceful couple you made!"

"Grandmama, perhaps you should not depend upon it too much," Pen suggested gently. "With so many persons in attendance, you cannot expect my cousin Owen will wish to partner me."

"Nonsense! Although, when I reflect upon who is

coming to our little party, I cannot resist a swell of pride. So many people, and quite a few nobility, are to attend, you know, and for that we may thank the regent. Once he decided to remain in town, all his hangers-on and followers decided to do so, as well, and they are the very people who shall fill our ballroom to capacity.''

In very little time Pen sought escape from her duties and the ever-prevailing subject of the ball. With Candace following close upon her heels, she went looking for Tom in the stables. She found, instead, that Owen was there. He had just returned from Town and had driven his curricle into the yard. He was engaged in the task of explaining to a groom that one of the wheels was a trifle loose when Candace ran up to him, wagging her tail and yapping several syllables in greeting.

''Mongrel dog!'' he said, as he bent over to scratch the precise spot behind her ears that he seemed to be able to find easily. ''No, don't jump up on me, or we shall both be made to suffer my valet's wrath!''

Pen laughed and Owen looked up immediately. A spark flamed to life in his eyes, and she felt her heart trip a little bit faster.

At first she wasn't sure if he would even speak to her, but he hesitated only a moment before he walked over to her with long-legged strides.

''Cousin!'' he said, rather coolly. ''What brings you here?''

''I was looking for Tom Hawkins. I meant to ask if I might resume my daily rides and . . .'' Uncertain of how to go on, she allowed her voice to trail away. She looked up into his face, hoping to see some sign, some hint, that he had forgiven her. She found none.

"I still ride in the morning," he said.

"Do you?" she asked, uncertain if she should interpret his cryptic remark as an invitation to join him or a warning to stay away. She waited for him to speak again, and when he didn't she said in some exasperation, "Owen, I wish you could bring yourself to trust me just a little again."

He didn't answer right away, but looked off into the distance, as if he were trying to form the right words.

She decided to do what she could to help him, and said, "Grandmama has her heart set upon seeing us dance again at the ball, just as we did at The Pavilion. Owen, I do not wish to disappoint her."

He looked at her then, and she saw the telltale pull of the muscle in his jaw. "I will, of course, do my duty to your grandmother."

"But I don't want you to dance with me out of duty, Owen! I want you to dance with me because you wish to!"

He looked away again. "You should have told me the truth. I would have protected you, Pen. I would have made sure no harm came to you. Why couldn't you have told me the truth?"

"I did, but you wouldn't listen to me."

He was looking at her, that odd sort of light again shining in the depths of his eyes. He wanted so much to believe her, but reason and common sense told him that he could not. She was standing there, looking at him in such a sad and rather earnest way that he was half tempted to take her in his arms and kiss her again until the worry was banished forever from her brow. The stablehands milling about nearby brought him back to his senses.

He said politely, "I won't disappoint your grandmother, Pen. Please put my name down on your card for the first dance."

He turned abruptly and walked back to the house, leaving Pen standing alone with Candace in the stable yard, sorely tempted to scream in frustration.

Owen entered the house to find Robert waiting for him in a somewhat agitated state.

"There you are, at last!" he exclaimed as Owen stripped off his gloves and hat and handed them to a waiting footman. "I've been looking for you an age!"

"And now you have found me," said Owen mildly. He opened a nearby door, saying "Shall we go into the library? What would you like—sherry?"

"Nothing, thank you. Owen, you might as well know I have come on a matter of great importance, and I'm—well, I'm deuced uncomfortable about the whole affair, I can tell you!"

"This sounds serious! What is it you have come to talk about?"

"First, let me say that you and I have been friends for some time now—years, in fact! And I've often thought that if ever I was in a fix, you would be the man I'd trust most to turn to. Do you understand what I'm saying to you?"

Owen frowned slightly and set down on the table the glass he had just poured. He said, quietly, "I do indeed understand, and I can assure you, you need say no more. Only tell me what trouble you are in, and I shall help in any way I can."

"Not me, dash it!" exclaimed Robert furiously. "I'm talking about you! I'm talking about the trouble you are in!"

"You mistake. I am not in any trouble whatsoever."

"Oh, yes, you are! And you needn't deny it to me— not your oldest and dearest friend. I know just what sort of predicament you have been in since your father died. Don't look at me that way, for I don't mean to hold it over your head! You've been doing your best these long months, and now—well, perhaps your best just isn't good enough anymore."

"Robert, what in blazes are you talking about?"

"I'm telling you that I know about the thefts."

There was a stunned silence.

"How do you know?" asked Owen, frowning in a manner that Robert considered with caution.

He said quickly, "I was in the jewelry shop when Pen pawned the ring you gave her."

"What ring? What jewelry shop?"

"Don't play coy with me, for I have already figured everything out for myself. I know you are The Black Bard, Owen, and I know, too, that Pen Hamilton is in league with you!"

If he hadn't been so surprised, Owen might have laughed. As it was, he could only stare at his friend until he managed to say, in a tone mixed of incredulity and outrage, "Have you lost your mind?"

"No, I haven't, and don't think for one minute that I made that accusation lightly. I know about your finances, for you've confided bits and pieces of your situation to me over the last year. And I know, too, that you share more than a coincidence worth of physical traits with that cursed highwayman. You both have dark hair, you both have light eyes, and then there's the fact that you are both known to be excellent horsemen—!"

"Then perhaps you'll be good enough to recall," interrupted Owen, "that The Black Bard was responsible for my father's death. Now, look me in the eye and tell me you think I could ever have had anything to do with such nefarious behavior!"

As this was a contingency Mr. Carswell had neglected to consider, he was not disposed to do any such thing. He hesitated, then said with healthy confusion, "Yes, well, I hadn't thought of that."

"It appears to me that there are any number of things you haven't thought of," said Owen. He returned his attention to the decanter of sherry, and this time he poured out a glass for his friend and handed it to him. "Now, suppose you tell me what prompted all of this."

Robert took a sip of sherry and told the story of Pen in the jeweler's shop.

Owen listened without emotion, but when the tale was finished he rubbed one hand across his jaw. "The little fool!"

"Yes. But if you are not The Black Bard, then where did Pen Hamilton get that ring? She had to have got it from the thief himself."

"Not necessarily. She could have got it from any number of people of her acquaintance, engaged in the very same occupation in which she—" He stopped short, and this time he rubbed both hands across his eyes. "I think you have just succeeded in confirming my worst fears."

"What do you mean?"

"I mean that Pen is a thief," said Owen as if the words were wrenched from his soul. "I should have known! Her first night here she spoke in almost glowing terms of having met that cursed highwayman! There were other signs as well, that I chose to ignore merely because she was pretty and endearing and had a certain charm about her."

"She's still rather charming," said Robert, "so much so that I find it hard to believe her capable of such crimes!"

"I have the same difficulty, I assure you!"

"What will you do about it, Owen?"

"First, I must swear you to secrecy. No one must know about this."

"You're protecting her, and not, I think, merely because she is family."

Owen took a sip from his glass and launched a rather quelling look across the rim at his friend. "You've already made one gross error in judgment this evening, Robert. I wouldn't recommend you make another."

"Don't waste your threats on me, thank you. I'm immune to them. Besides, I'd have to be daft as a brush not to see you're halfway in love with the girl."

"Stubble it! Do I have your word, or not?"

"You have it, for all the good it shall do you. Sooner or later someone is bound to notice things missing."

"The family is already suspicious, but not of her. I suppose if no one is to know, I shall just have to keep a close watch Pen Hamilton from this moment on."

Chapter Thirteen

Mrs. Kendrick predicted that her ball was to be a decided success. Each member of her family, she noted, was in fine looks. Her table, under Beardsley's unstinting eye, had been set for forty places with her best damask and china. And her ballroom, thanks to Pen's diligence, resembled something on the order of a fairyland.

She lacked only the presence of the regent to make the entire evening the envy of all her acquaintances, but Peter had assured her that such a dream was not meant to come true. Still, she could not find fault with her guest list, and when the appointed hour of eight o'clock at last arrived she greeted each guest with a swelling heart that threatened to bubble over.

The most glittering persons of Brighton society climbed the steps to the front hall of Rosemount. Beardsley ushered them up the stairs in his most

imposing manner. Two footmen and two maids collected their capes and coats. Additional footmen
posted at the landing ensured that no hapless new-
comer should suffer the embarrassment of getting
lost in the numerous passageways of the great manor
house.

Owen and Peter stood by to help Mrs. Kendrick
receive her guests. Pen and Augusta together mingled
among the visitors.

More guests arrived, among them, Robert Carswell,
who shook hands with his hostess and offered a curt
nod toward Owen. His eyes scanned the room, searching out Augusta. He found her and went to her
straightaway. She raised her blue eyes toward his, and
cast him a look of strained hopefulness.

He pressed her hand. "You'll forgive me, Miss
Hamilton, if I take Augusta away for a moment. I
have to speak with her—now! Urgently! I'll bring her
back in a whisper!" he said, as he led her a little bit
away from the other guests.

Beardsley announced dinner shortly after eight
o'clock, a fact which greatly gratified Mrs. Kendrick.
She led the way into the dining room on the arm of
a cabinet minister, and the rest of her guests paired
off and followed suit.

Pen found herself seated at dinner between two
very attentive partners, each of whom proved adept at
maintaining rather one-sided conversations on their
own which required very little participation on her
part. That, she thought, was just as well, for her
thoughts were on Owen throughout the meal. Several
times she looked down the length of the table to find

that he was watching her, but in the light of the candles she could not tell if his expression held approval or censure.

The ball was to begin at ten o'clock, and after leaving the dinner table Pen thought she had some time for solitude before the dancing commenced. She was unsure if Owen would ask to partner her in a dance, and equally unsure of how he would treat her if he did. She didn't think she could bear to have him hold her in his arms and gaze down upon her with that cold, rather unfeeling expression he had worn ever since the night of the regent's ball. When she chanced to think that she might never again feel the warmth of his embrace or the sweet crush of his lips against hers, she found that she was hovering perilously close to tears.

She wanted to escape for a mere moment or two to a quiet place in which she might compose herself. She left the public rooms and was making her way past the library when the door flew open and Owen was suddenly standing there before her.

He seemed just as surprised to see her as she was to see him, but after a moment he said, "Pen! I was just about to call for you. Will you do me the favor of stepping inside?"

She did as he asked and found Robert Carswell already in the room. He stood up at her entrance, but there was no trace of his usual friendly smile. Rather, he was wearing an expression of grave injury that was not unlike the same expression Owen wore.

"Please sit down, Pen," Owen said, holding a chair for her. "I think you should be comfortable, for we have some business to discuss and I think it shall prove to be a somewhat lengthy interview.''

Her eyes darted from Owen's face to Robert's, then back. "What is it? Has something gone wrong?"

"Something has, indeed. Someone present at dinner tonight has taken advantage of our guests and robbed them."

"I don't believe it!" she said, visibly stunned.

"It's true," said Robert. "I discovered the deed myself when I went looking for my snuff box. I had left it in the pocket of my great coat, and when I went to look for it it was gone."

"There are other things missing, as well from our guests—a fur-lined cape belonging to the cabinet minister, a gold lorgnette belonging to Lady Ambersleigh."

"But this is dreadful!" uttered Pen. "What do you think is to be done?"

"Nothing need be done," said Owen. "In fact, this business can remain a secret held between just the three of us. It only remains that you tell me what you did with the things you stole."

"The things *I* stole?" she repeated incredulously.

"Do not look to play games with me," he warned, "for I know very well that you are responsible!"

"But I am not!" she said, leaping to her feet. She took an agitated turn about the room. "I have told you before, Owen Kendrick, I am not a thief. Why will you not believe me?"

"I'd like to, Pen. God knows I want to! But the truth of the matter is that none of these thefts occurred before you came to Rosemount and—! Pen, I know all about the ring you pawned.''

That simple statement brought her steps to a sudden and complete halt. "How do you know about that?"

"I was there, Miss Hamilton," said Robert. "I was in the shop when you came in. I saw you make the transaction with my own eyes."

She brought her hands up to cover her cheeks, which had lost their usually healthy color. "Oh, God, now I am completely undone!" she uttered miserably.

Owen took her hands in his and said in a gentle tone, "No, you are not. I told you before I would protect you, and the offer still stands. Only tell me where you have hidden the things you took, and no harm shall come to you, I swear it!"

"But that's just it—I didn't take them." She saw a look of frustration cross Owen's face and she said, hastily, "I swear to you I have never stolen anything in my life but—but I have done something far, far worse!" She took momentary comfort in the feeling of Owen's strong hands clasping hers, but she had a feeling that she might never know such comfort again. She squared her shoulders and said bravely, "Owen, I didn't steal those things, but I think I know who did! In fact, I am certain of it. Please, you must let me go so I may see if my suspicions are correct."

Owen studied her face a moment before he released her. "Very well, but you must return to this room within five minutes, or I shall come looking for you. Do you understand? Swear to me now! Say you will return in five minutes."

"I won't fail you," she promised, for she knew in her heart that Owen would never give her another chance. Only now would she be able to prove to him that she was not the thief he imagined her to be.

She left the library for what she hoped would be her last journey to the farthest bedchamber in the old east wing. As she made her way down the passage she could hear the music coming from the ballroom along with the din of chattering guests. She kept moving down the passage. At the door to the bedchamber she rapped lightly, but received no answer.

She cracked the door open slightly. "James? James, it is I, Pen," she called, but still she received no response. She opened the door a little wider and slipped into the room.

A single candle was burning very low in a brass lamp near the window. It proved to be the only source of light in the room, but the light it cast was sufficient for Pen to notice that something was different about the place.

The trunks and chests that James had collected were placed against one wall, much as they had been when last she had seen them. She was certain that when she had seen them before their drawers had been pulled and their doors ajar, so that even the most casual observer could see the riches and treasures they held. On this evening, however, the compartments had been shut and the trunks and chests were neatly closed, as if their owner were ready to send them on a journey.

A portion of the bandboxes she had seen before were gone, too, as well as the jewel-encrusted enamel box that had caught Pen's eye when last she had been in the room.

"James?" she called again, willing him to appear. In vain did she wait for him to answer, and she knew in her heart that he was gone. From the appearance of the room she knew, too, that he had every intention of returning to retrieve the rest of his belongings.

Her heart sank. Without James she would never be able to prove to Owen that she had not stolen the items stowed in the bedchamber. Without James, he would never believe that she was not the thief of his imaginings.

She turned to snuff the candle out, and as she did so a movement outside the window caught her eye. In the darkness she could just make out the figure of a man walking across the lawns. He was carrying a large bundle over his shoulder, and he was heading in the direction of the stable.

She hurried back down to the library. She passed by the drawing room where Candace was dozing by the fire. Attracted by Pen's hurried steps, Candace let out a shrill yap of enjoyment and joined her.

When at last she reached the library, Pen opened the door and rushed into the room. "Hurry! You must follow me to the stables and quickly, for there is no time to waste!"

"Pen, what is it?" demanded Owen as he clasped her hand and held it fast. "Tell me what is going on. You look as though you have been running."

"I have, but that is of no matter. What is important is that we must go to the stables. Please, come with me!" she begged with such urgency that Owen immediately ushered her through the door—with Robert and Candace following close behind.

As they hurried across the lawns Pen prayed that they would not be too late, that James would not have already made his escape.

"Hurry!" she adjured them.

"Perhaps you had better tell me what we are doing out here, Pen," Owen suggested.

"There is no time, I'm afraid. Look, we are nearly at the stable, and I can see no one about! I fear we have arrived too late, after all!"

"Too late for what, Miss Hamilton?" asked Robert. "I agree with Owen. I think it is time you came clean and told us the truth."

They reached the stables and rounded the side of the stalls. To her vast relief James was there in the stable yard, busily saddling Little Angel. At his feet was a knapsack—filled, she thought, with pilfered treasures. He saw them approach from the corner of his eye and calmly trained a pistol upon them.

They stopped in their tracks. Candace let out several yaps of alarm, and Robert scooped her up and held her tightly in his arms.

"Pen," said Owen, cautiously, "be so good as to get behind me."

Slowly, she did as he said, and when he knew she was no longer in any direct line of fire, he said quite calmly to the gunman, "I don't know who you are. Perhaps I can persuade you to put the gun down."

"I think not. My freedom is too important to me not to insure a safe escape. I do thank you, however, for your hospitality, for I have enjoyed staying at

Rosemount. I have even collected some mementos to take with me," he added, and he nudged the knapsack with his boot.

"Your stay at Rosemount?" Owen repeated. "What do you mean?"

"Didn't our little brown wren tell you? Thanks to her tender mercies and ministrations, I have been a guest of yours in a fine bedchamber in the east wing of the house."

From her vantage point behind him, Pen saw Owen's shoulders stiffen. He said, in a rather ominous tone, "Pen, do you know this man?"

For a moment she was too mortified to speak, but she had pledged that Owen would have the truth, and she didn't think there was any point in turning back now. She took a step from behind Owen, the better to see his expression, and said, "Yes, Owen, I do. This is James, but I think you know him better by his other name. You see, he calls himself The Black Bard."

"And you," said James, "must be the famous Owen Kendrick. So, at last we meet! Yes, go ahead, all of you and have a good long look at my face without the mask. It will do you no good to try to memorize my features, for I assure you, I intend to kill you before you ever have a chance to describe my likeness to a magistrate."

Pen took a step toward him, and demanded in a voice of deep injury, "How could you do this? How could you steal from me and my family and then threaten our very lives?"

"Pray, don't behave so surprised, my dear girl. You

did know I was a thief before you took me in," he said, clearly unrepentant.

"But to repay me thus? I was kind to you and nursed you and incurred Owen's wrath for you!"

"But you did much more than that!" he assured her. "After all, it was you who told me where the treasure is."

"I never did any such thing!" she exclaimed.

"Ah, but you did. In the midst of your misguided attempts to help me, you explained to me what a bearer bond was. Having never learned to read, I would never have known what was written on those papers I stole so long ago. God knows why I ever kept them in the first place, but I did, and I have them with me now, and I mean to make them good."

"But you told me you didn't have them any more," Pen sputtered indignantly. "You told me you thought they were garbage, and had discarded them long ago!"

"It pains me to admit it, but I lied to you," he said, with perfect aplomb.

"And did you lie about everything? Did you lie when you said all those things to me? When you paid sweet compliments to me and—and kissed me?"

He smiled then, a slight smile that held a wealth of contempt. "It is time you learned a lesson in life— no man who kisses a woman does so in all honesty. Tell me truthfully, did you actually think you and I would ever have any sort of life together? You are either the most innocent girl alive, or the most foolish!"

He finished buckling the saddle on Little Angel's

back and gathered up the sack of stolen treasures. With the pistol still trained on Owen, he fitted his boot into the stirrup and started to hoist himself up onto the horse's back.

Just then Candace took exception to his tone.

She yapped excitedly; she leveraged her hind legs against Robert's chest and gave a mighty push. She sprang forward out of his arms and nipped at the highwayman's heel as it left the ground.

Little Angel skittered to her right, and Candace let out another yap of ferocious proportions for a dog of her size.

James clung to the pommel, one foot trapped in the stirrup, and one poised in midair. He let out a ringing oath. Even as the word left his mouth, he lost his balance and Owen, with lightning reflexes, pounced on him.

He wrested James from the horse as Robert grabbed at the gun in his hand. James struggled, but Owen had the advantage of height and weight, and before the highwayman had had a chance to regain his balance Owen leveled him with a single blow to his chin.

The gun went flying as James sprawled indelicately on the ground. He struggled to get up, only to find that Owen had planted his boot in the middle of his chest.

"After what you have done to my family, I could squash you right now like the bug you are," said Owen.

Pen placed a restraining hand on his arm. "Please! Please don't endanger yourself. If you seek your revenge you shall only end up facing a charge of murder. Please, Owen, do not hurt him, I beg you!"

He didn't react immediately, but after a moment in which he had an opportunity to judge the prudence of her words he removed his booted foot from atop the highwayman's chest. "We'll take him to the local magistrate and ensure he is safely locked away with no possibility of escape. Pen, be so good as to hand me one of the training ropes hanging in the empty stall."

She quickly did as he asked and watched him use the rope to bind James at his ankles and wrists.

"I'm coming with you," Pen said impetuously.

"Oh, no, you're not," retorted Robert with an eye to keeping the pistol trained on James. "You must stay here, Miss Hamilton, and take the dog back inside with you."

"He's right, Pen," Owen said. "You must stay here. Your grandmother might notice your absence and send someone to look for you."

She didn't wish to be left behind, but she recognized the wisdom of his words. "You will be careful, won't you?" she asked.

"Pen, don't tease yourself with worry. I'll return, but you must go back into the house now and behave before your grandmother and her guests as if nothing has gone amiss tonight."

Compared to watching Owen prepare to transport a known criminal with little more than a horse and a single weapon, she thought that hers must be the easier task. She was wrong. For no sooner did she scoop Candace up in her arms and make her way back into the house than she found that she could not bring herself to return to the ballroom and behave as if nothing untoward had occurred.

Chapter Fourteen

Upon his return Owen found Pen in one of the bedchambers in the east wing. She didn't notice his presence at first, so busy was she at her task. She was surrounded by the trunks and chests that James had accumulated in his room and she was engaged in the business of searching each item that had once belonged to him.

Owen watched her for a few moments and felt his temper rise. He stepped into the room and asked, somewhat bitingly, "Looking for a memento, are you?"

Startled, she turned quickly and saw that he was advancing upon her. In his hand was the knapsack of stolen items they had left earlier in the stable yard.

She felt foolishly overjoyed to see him. Since she had returned to the house, her imagination had run rampant, imagining that one outlandish fate after another had befallen Owen and Robert. In her heart she believed that delivering James to the magistrate was a much more dangerous task than Owen had been willing to allow. When she saw that his handsome face was marred by a decided frown she knew he did not feel the same joy in seeing her. He hadn't yet forgiven her, she realized, but she didn't think now was the time for her to put her pride above her heart. If need be, she was willing to beg him to reconsider.

"Owen," she said rather tentatively, "I . . . I have decided to confess the whole to you. I . . . I brought him here. It was all my doing. He was hurt—shot, Tom said!—and I couldn't leave him to die in the meadow. Tom Hawkins helped me, but he isn't to blame, for I swore him to secrecy. I simply wanted to keep James here until his shoulder could heal. It was naive of me—I know that now, but I swear I never dreamed he would take advantage—! To think that he actually moved his stolen treasures in—!"

He grasped her by the shoulders then, bringing her rambling and somewhat disjointed speech to an end.

"Just tell me one thing," he said as he looked her in the eye with a penetrating gaze. "Were you in love with him?"

She shook her head sorrowfully. "No, but I admit I was infatuated at first. He seemed so dashing, and I was so foolish."

"You said earlier that he kissed you."

"Yes, once," she answered wretchedly, "and I know now that it was wrong of me to have let him do so."

"Thank you, my dear. I believe that is all you need

say." And with those words, he promptly pulled her into his arms and kissed her soundly.

This time she didn't struggle against him, but allowed him to kiss her, and she even ventured so far as to reach her hand up to his shoulder and somewhat tentatively return his embrace.

When at last he raised his head she asked, "Are you not angry with me?"

"I am furious!" he said in a cordial tone.

"I deceived you shamefully!" she added for good measure, in case he had not yet realized the full extent of her crimes.

"I am well aware of that, thank you."

"I wish you would not speak so nonsensically when I am endeavoring to be serious. I treated you badly, Owen, and for that at the very least I deserve some sort of punishment!"

"You are right, of course. And I think I shall begin punishing you now." Once again his lips closed over hers, this time in an exquisite kiss that was, to Pen, more like heaven than any form of punishment had a right to be.

Some time later, after having kissed Pen often and most thoroughly, Owen asked, "Tell me, what were you doing rummaging through those trunks when I came in earlier?"

"I was looking for the bearer bonds. James lied to me, you know. He said he didn't have the wretched things."

Owen picked up the sack of treasures he had brought with him from the stables and deposited it upon the bed. He untied the knot and spread back the cloth to reveal a myriad of rings, brooches, watches, and silver coins. Amid all those things was a thick sheaf of papers. He held it aloft, smiling, his blue eyes alight with a keenness she had never seen there before.

"I have them!" he said triumphantly. "I have the bonds, thank God!"

"Is it true? Are they all there?"

He picked her up in his arms and swung her dizzyingly about until she let out a shriek of pleasure. "What if I were to tell you that we shall spend the first days of our lives together counting them, if you like?"

"I should say that I like that idea very much," she answered, smiling.

"And if some of the notes and bonds are missing, I won't repine. If our family fortune cannot be fully restored, at least we are guaranteed to be on a surer footing than we were before."

"Perhaps then you will no longer feel compelled to carry the weight of the world on your shoulders."

"Perhaps, but as long as I have a wife who insists upon helping other people and prying into affairs that are no concern of hers, I fear I am destined to spend my days worrying."

"Wouldn't you rather spend your time helping others? Only consider Augusta and Robert Carswell! How splendid it would be if they were to marry at long last."

"They will, mark my words. If I have to march them down the aisle at gunpoint, I swear I shall see them married and happy! Now, will you kindly cease meddling?''

Pen giggled. ''Not yet. I was thinking that Tom Hawkins appeared to me to be a rather lonely man. You know, if only he had a wife—''

''If he had a wife, he still would not be as happy as you and I,'' interrupted Owen with authority. ''I love you, Pen Hamilton. Now, tell me you feel the same and be quick, for in case you have forgotten you and I have a ball to attend.''

ABOUT THE AUTHOR

Nancy Lawrence lives with her family in Aurora, CO, and is the author of five Zebra Regency romances. She loves to hear from readers, and you may write to her c/o Zebra Books. Please include a self-addressed stamped envelope if you wish a response.